THE HAMMER OF THOR

THE HAMMER OF THOR

The Phoenix Quest Series
#1

K.T. TOMB

The Hammer of Thor

Published by K.T. Tomb
Copyright © 2013 by K.T. Tomb

ISBN 13: 9781494788247
ISBN: 1494788241

ACCLAIM FOR K.T. TOMB:

"Epic and awesome!"
—**J.T. Cross**, bestselling author of *Beneath the Deep*

"Now *this* is what I call adventure. *The Lost Garden* will leave you breathless!"
—**Summer Lee**, bestselling author of *Angel Heart*

"The best adventure novel I've read in a long time. K.T. Tomb. I can't wait to read the sequel. Count me a fan. A *big* fan."
—**P.J. Day**, bestselling author of *The Sunset Prophecy*

"K.T. Tomb is a wonderful new voice in adventure fiction. I was enthralled by *The Lost Garden*...and you will be, too."
—**Aiden James**, bestselling author of *Plague of Coins*

OTHER BOOKS BY
K.T. TOMB

STANDALONE ADVENTURES
The Last Crusade
The Tempest
The Adventurers
Sasquatch Mountain

THE EVAN KNIGHT ADVENTURES
The Lost Garden
Keepers of the Lost Garden
Destroyers of the Lost Garden

THE PHOENIX QUEST ADVENTURES
The Hammer of Thor
The Spear of Destiny
The Lair of Beowulf

THE CHYNA STONE ADVENTURES
The Minoan Mask
The Mummy Codex
The Phoenician Falcon

THE CASH CASSIDY ADVENTURES
The Holy Grail
The Lost Continent
The Lost City of Gold

THE EVA HEART THRILLERS
The Lucifer Legion
The God Game
The Archangel Agenda

THE ASIA SHANE THRILLERS
The Staff
The Order
The Plague

THE ALAN QUATERMAIN ADVENTURES
The Road to Shambala
The Seal of Solomon
The Shroud of Turin

DEDICATION

The author wishes to dedicate this book to
Michael Crichton.

CHAPTER ONE

Phoe stood with her back pressed flat against the one hundred-foot wall facing the Amazon River in Iquitos City, Peru. Her emerald eyes were on fire as she pushed her sandy blond hair away from her face.

Stone steps separated the wall's expanse, forty feet apart, roughly twenty feet lower than the last. The giant stone staircase would be impossible for a normal-sized person to descend, if not for the low-hanging vines from the heavy canopy of trees adjacent to the walkway.

"It's not a coincidence that the vines are here, Jonathan!" Phoe barked to a nervous young man standing on the top step at the wall's highest point. "This was planned so people could use them to climb. It doesn't happen by accident!"

"I don't know," he replied, his knees shaking. "It looks like an easy way to die!"

She stood perched on the third step down, irritated that he was too frightened to move. "I'd really like to talk about the laws of physics with you in more detail, but in case you haven't noticed, we're running out of time!"

"I'm serious Phoe!" pleaded Jonathon. "This circus act is a little much for me."

"Well, sweetheart, unless you can get a grip on your fear of heights, I'll have to assume that you'll soon be out of the running for this little adventure, huh?"

"Did anyone ever comment on how you play horribly with others?" he asked, sarcastically.

"You mean, you're just now figuring out that I get more accomplished on my own, and that other people usually just get in my way?" she shot back.

"Like who?" He feigned a wound to his male pride.

"Like you, silly! But seriously, either you get your shit together or I'm going to drop you off some place. It's turning out to be one of my worst decisions."

"Why did you bring me, then?"

"Your father happens to be a valued client. He expects me to bring you back alive."

"Hey, I'm helping you find the...."

She cut him a look to shut him up. "Seriously, if you want to live, do what I tell you, Jonathan. Period."

"Fine."

A dark-haired figure stood thirty feet away, on the other side of the river. Peter Kellerman waved to her, grinning in a gloating way. She fought the urge to wave back with one finger. Peter and Phoe had been friends since high school, in Albuquerque, New Mexico. Phoe had carried her rebellious nature, going so far as to change her name after graduation. Named after her grandmother, she decided to stop answering to her formal name, and would no longer acknowledge it, ever. She preferred to simply be known as Phoe, which was short for her last name, Phoenix. Ever since, Peter would bring up her real first name every now and then, perhaps to keep it as a bargaining chip.

Having spurned his advances long ago, she understood his need to compete with her at every opportunity. Like right then. When she excelled in track in high school, he took up running. When she took gymnastics, he immediately followed suit. When she got interested in hunting down and collecting artifacts, he made it his life's mission to beat her at her own game.

"Do you have a reason for that evil grin on your face, Peter?" she called across the river.

"Why do you assume my grin is evil?" he called back.

The thing about him that irritated her most was the fact he used the word *assume* more than most people. "Because I know your smiles and this is one I enjoy the least!"

"Ah, come on, Phoe," he teased. "Or should I share an embarrassing secret with the dude about to pee his pants over there?"

"Don't you dare!" she warned.

"Your dilemma is heartrending—truly it is. Use the vines to come over and shut me up. Or, better yet...try to stop me before I find the..." He held up a silver jaguar's head about the size of a bowling ball. Its dark jeweled eyes glistened in the sun. "Oops, too late...again! Looks like I already located the *Head of Olmec!* Beaten again...Imagine that!"

"No!" she shouted angrily.

He laughed, obviously tickled by the upper hand he had gained. "Truly, I feel your pain, sis. If you come after me to try to take the Head of Olmec, you won't be able to get back there to save your man in distress. What to do, *oh my*, what to do?...Well, I wish I could stay and chat, but surely you realize I have to take my shiny new friend someplace warm and dry!"

"He's got it! He's got the Head of Olmec in his hand! I can't believe it!" Jonathan exclaimed, as if only suddenly aware of what presently transpired between Peter and Phoe.

"Concentrate on not falling, would you?" said Phoe, glancing back at Jonathan, before returning her attention to Peter.

Of all the shit Peter had pulled on her, he picked a terrible time to be cute. She began the silent debate about what her client would miss more: the Head of Olmec or his precious son. Meanwhile, Peter made his getaway, disappearing into the jungle. At the same time, the massive stone steps began to retract into the wall. A straight drop into piranha-infested waters was a small fact she had omitted from Jonathon's awareness, for understandable reasons. But, time to rescue him would run out soon.

She grabbed the nearest vine and took a three-step lunge to start the pendulum process of swinging back and forth, hoping to gain enough momentum to reach the top step. Jonathan suddenly noticed the disappearing ledge he was perched upon, whimpering for her to save his ass. *Easy does it, Mr. Kessler...two more swings and I'll....*

He prepared to dive.

"Don't do it, Jonathon!"

"Why? How deep is the river?"

"Deep enough! Don't jump unless you want to be eaten by piranhas!"

"What?!" he cried out in surprise.

"Yes, piranhas!" she confirmed, while trying to align herself with where he stood.

"Oh, shit!"

The ledge pushed him to the edge. He started to fall.

"Gotcha!" She grabbed onto him, but only had a moment for him to adjust. He had better listen, or they both would be piranha chow in a moment. "Grab onto the vine—I've got you!"

Phoe had just turned twenty-five. The age when things get clearer for most young people, after school, lost friends, and opportunities and regrets from the past are let go, and hope spurs the mindful few to greater things in life. That was her....Her trial and error adventures were like the early stages of a rocket being shed during lift off. As long as she didn't die right then.

Jonathon finally listened and, to her surprise, bravely wrapped himself—hands, arms, and legs—tightly around the vine while she continued to hang on to him. But that was just part one of this crazy exercise.

"Hold on!"

"I am, damn it!"

Perhaps he thought she would aim for the trees, and they would then either try to scale them to reach the wall and continue their climb at impossible odds, or they could slide to the ground and start over...or go back from whence they came. Or....

"Holy shit! Are you insane?!" he shrieked.

"Maybe!"

Phoe arched back while hovering dangerously over the river far below. Leaning back dangerously while Jonathon continued to panic. He kept screaming until they reached the very top of the wall.

"Drop—*now!*"

It was an act of faith. Not for her...but for him. Even as she skidded across the rough rock surface, picking up bruises and painful scrapes as she tumbled, she managed to look back. For an instant, she didn't see him, and thought he had fallen into the river, to a horrific death. But then he landed on top of her with a crunching thud.

"Aww...shit! Do you mind?" she scolded him, throwing him dangerously close to the edge until she dragged him back to safety.

Both gasped for breath. When calm enough to move again, she released a huge sigh of relief. Jonathon let out a whoop and holler toward the sky above.

"We made it!" he enthused.

"We did," she agreed, allowing a brief smile in celebration that they remained among the living. But soon the elation faded at the realization they remained in a pickle, while good ole Peter slipped further away.

Returning home victorious, to Taos, New Mexico, seemed increasingly unlikely.

"Now, how do we get down from here, Phoe?" Jonathon asked, his earlier joy evaporating as he tentatively gazed at the river farther below them, and glancing at the rugged terrain to cross through on the other side of the wall.

"That, my friend, remains the sixty-thousand dollar question." She allowed her smirk to broaden into a playful smile, and slapped him on the back.

Time to get going.

Chapter Two

It was a quiet day for Charlotte DeCampos, a friend of Phoe's mother's who had agreed to look after the shop when Phoe was away.

She applied herself to learning every aspect of Simple Treasures. She recalled helping Phoe build the handmade shelves. In fact, it was her idea to make the shop look like a log cabin. She enjoyed managing the inventory, especially the arrowheads, fossils, and well-made replicas of Greek, Roman, and Italian artifacts.

Charlotte was also the one to find a specialist who knew how to copy artifacts. Almost every time Phoe went on one of her quests, she brought back something rare and unusual. Making replicas for Phoe to sell helped keep the shop in the black. The two women shared the house connected to the back of the shop—and not so much for financial considerations as it was Phoe's general mistrust of strangers, and wanting to keep a close eye on her store.

Charlotte also liked to take credit for talking Phoe into moving to Taos, New Mexico in the first place. Perfectly located in northern New Mexico, gaining access to the surrounding area rich in history, culture and people who could afford her artifacts was an easy deal.

Presently, it had been a slow week. Charlotte was painting her nails when a stranger arrived, hoping to see Phoe. The man stood impatiently at the counter, repeatedly checking his watch. In his late forties, the well-groomed gentleman in an expensive tailored suit huffed loud enough for Charlotte to pause and look up at him.

"Like I said, she should be here any time," said Charlotte. "You sure you don't want a cup of coffee while you wait?"

"No," he responded, tersely.

Charlotte braced herself for another serving of the man's speech about his time wasted while waiting amounted to more than she'd make in the coming year. Thankfully, however, Phoe and Jonathan burst through the front door. Running late left her boss in a cloudy mood, or maybe it was the sling on Phoe's right arm.

"What in the hell happened?" Charlotte nearly spilled her bottle of nail polish as she ran from behind the desk to assist her boss, "I'm fine, Charlotte," said Phoe, her brow furrowed as she looked past her to their visitor. "It's just a precaution. Gotta love those doctors."

"You have a visitor, Phoe," whispered Charlotte. "He doesn't want to tell me his name."

The well-dressed man turned around, raising an eyebrow in concern. "Jonathan. Are you all right?"

"Yeah, Dad, I think so." Jonathan smiled weakly.

"Phoe, we have things to discuss. I prefer someplace private," said Simon Kessler.

Phoe motioned for him to follow her to her office. Kessler's eyes studied the room, and he smirked as his gaze fell upon the mess of paperwork and empty chocolate milk containers on her desk.

"We have to talk, Phoe," he said. "The mission was an utter failure."

"That depends on what you consider a failure," she said. She motioned for him to a chair across from hers and they sat down together. "Your son came back in one piece. In fact, it was because of saving him that I lost the Head of Olmec."

"I would appreciate if you wouldn't blame your inadequacies on Jonathan."

"If Jonathan wasn't shadowing me, then I would have the Olmec. Simple as that. How exactly would you like me to rephrase the facts? You may be paying my expenses, but in order for things to work out as they should, you have to let me do what I do alone. Unencumbered."

"What you do alone? Yet, you lack the academic degrees and experience to have earned that privilege. As I feared, your inexperience cost you the Olmec, which is *not* why I funded the expedition!"

"And yet, you hired me anyway. Spit it out, Simon. You knew I would fail, and that your son would be a liability. Cut the shit and tell me what your game is."

Kessler reached into his coat pocket and pulled out a piece of paper.

"Have you seen this? It's from a Swedish online news source." He handed her a folded slip of paper. She read it and tossed it on the desk, unimpressed.

"You do realize it's an April Fool's joke right? It even states this fact beneath the article, 'April Fool's.' I saw this thing when it came out the first time. Don't tell me that the great billionaire Simon Kessler has been fooled by something so crazy."

"I'm not stupid, Phoe. I know a practical joke." He picked up the piece of paper and returned it to his pocket. "But this isn't entirely a joke. Too bad you can't read between the lines worth a damn."

She took the bait.

"Okay, what? Fine, you got me, Simon. But before you try to entice me with some new pot of gold at the end of a rainbow, you need to state clearly what's now in it for me. The ante's been upped. Way up."

Simon smiled. "On the contrary, Phoe. At last count, since you failed the Olmec mission, you owe me just over forty-five thousand dollars."

"What?! You're frigging crazy!" She got up and headed for the door.

"Take this on and your entire debt to me will be erased…"

She paused to listen.

"And, whether you find anything or not, you won't have to pay me back for *any* expenses you accrue."

She turned around, holding him in her gaze. "All right. But this time, I want you to give me a credit card with no limit for expenses. Put me on an account as an authorized user if you must. And, I want you to sign a contract stating what you just said. Also, none of your cronies come with me—not even your son. If I decide to take anyone, he or she will be my exclusive pick."

It took him a moment to respond, and for a moment he simply stared at her.

She began to fidget. "Simon, I'm a busy woman. You have exactly twenty seconds to take my offer or get the hell out of here."

A slight smile pulled at the corners of his mouth. "So, I am to be given an ultimatum? Good day to you, Phoe."

He left her office first, and when Phoe came out a minute later, she looked shock that Simon and Jonathan Kessler were long gone. Charlotte's response announced she just realized the closed-door meeting hadn't gone as well as her boss would've liked. Charlotte pursued Phoe into her office.

"Simon was smiling when he left. Did you two make a deal?" She said this sweetly while handing Phoe a twenty-ounce bottle of chocolate milk.

Phoe forced a sad smile, but her bottom lip quivered. Charlotte watched her move to close up the store for the evening. Phoe then grabbed the DVD copy of *Raiders of the Lost Ark*—one of her personal favorite movies—and moved past her to the living area of the hybrid house. Charlotte pursued her and placed the

DVD in the player when Phoe plopped down on the couch and buried her face in her hands.

Phoe began to weep, and as Charlotte moved to comfort her, she was pushed away.

"I owe Simon Kessler forty-five thousand dollars!" she sobbed. "How am I ever going to be able to pay him?"

CHAPTER THREE

A restless night awaited Phoe as she lay in bed. Watching *Raiders of the Lost Ark* hadn't eased her worries. Where in the hell would she come up with Kessler's money? For a moment, her heart lifted at the thought of not having a legal binding contract. She never signed anything. However, from her limited experience as a businesswoman, she knew that if a plaintiff could prove that certain expenses, or damages, were incurred, she would be on the hook for it all. Legally, Kessler's high-priced lawyers could very well end up taking Simple Treasures from her. If that happened, she would be royally screwed. Moving back in with her mother was akin to the 'March of Bataan' in her mind.

Maybe that was what she should do, anyway. Hell, she could start a store online and sell her artifact replicas without worrying about the overhead of a physical store. But, not wanting to lose something she had worked so hard to get, she started thinking long and hard about Kessler's proposal. She wondered if he truly planned to pursue what he had hinted at. Not caring for his arrogance, she acknowledged the fact he was highly intelligent, if not delusional. Played her coyly, too…as he had never come out and said what he wanted her to find. Instead, she saw it in his eyes—that childlike fascination.

Since Kessler had never specifically mentioned the artifact, she couldn't bring herself to say it out loud either. The notion was one beyond ridiculous. *He did say he would erase my debt whether I found it or not.* It would certainly be the latter, since how could she find something from the land of make-believe? Still, the 'all expenses paid tag' gave her pause to consider. After all, as a newbie in this biz, she didn't have a reputation to worry about ruining. Not yet.

Realizing she had nothing to lose by accepting the task, she started to smile. She could even request an advance, along with her demands. Hell the entire prospectus could be one long demand. That thought especially made her feel good and she chuckled as she climbed out of the depressive funk she'd been in since that afternoon.

She decided to watch a little television to help her fall asleep, now that her mind was at ease. All the while her mind kept returning to her favorite scene from *Raiders of the Lost Ark.* Where the angelic guardians melted the evil Nazis. Picturing screams of the unjust getting punished, something about the job offer from Kessler hit her, like a lead-filled boxing glove to the face.

"Oh my God, that's it!" she shouted in joyful surprise "Why in the hell didn't I connect it before….*Shit,* I've been so stupid!"

Still tender from the latest expedition, Phoe climbed out of bed and slowly made her way to a small desk in her bedroom, powering on her computer. Once on the Internet, she typed in 'Thor' and 'Nazis'.

"There it is," she whispered, almost reverently. "Oh…my…*God!*"

Finding sleep would prove difficult, still, but for a different reason.

"A 'forty-five thousand and then some' different reason," she said, pulling the covers back up once she climbed back in bed. It was the central theme of what floated through her mind, until the rest she longed for finally came.

CHAPTER FOUR

Phoe awoke to the smell of Charlotte's homemade buttermilk waffles and eggs over-easy, making her feel like a child again. A good memory of her mother's cooking and she loved the way the smell permeated the house.

She got dressed and practically ran to the dining room table. Charlotte sat at the table eating breakfast, having already set a place for Phoe.

Charlotte looked up and eyed her curiously.

"What?" Phoe returned her look with a suspicious one.

"Sorry, Phoe. You look radiant this morning."

"Well, I feel radiant," she said, sliding into her seat. She smiled impishly. "I'm going to call Simon Kessler and accept that impossible job."

She grabbed a waffle and took a big bite.

"What made you change your mind?"

"He didn't come out and say it, but I think Simon wants me to find Thor's Hammer."

Charlotte's mouth dropped open. She started to say something, but caught herself.

"I'm sorry. Did you say the Hammer of Thor?" she asked, wearing a look of disbelief.

"Sounds totally absurd, doesn't it?" Phoe paused to sip her coffee. "But, yes…he's willing to pay me to find what may or may not exist. The Hammer of Thor."

"Wait, wait a minute, kiddo." Charlotte eyed her like Phoe's mother often did, one eyebrow raised. "If he hasn't actually mentioned it by name, how do you know it's what he wants?"

"Trust me, Char. I've been doing this for a while now. I'd bet everything I have in the store right now that I'm right about this."

"Can I call the store Needful Things if I win?"

"Very funny," said Phoe, a bite of waffle drizzling syrup back onto her plate as she regarded her pal, and wearing a near-identical scornful look. "Are you saying that I'm not successful?"

"How exactly would you describe the word 'successful,' dear? I'm just being honest."

Phoe's cell phone chirped, and she waved off Charlotte to answer it, pausing only to wipe stickiness from her fingers.

"Simple Treasures, Phoe speaking."

"Good morning, Phoe. Simon Kessler here."

"Good morning, Simon." Phoe winked at Charlotte.

"I have considered your offer….I accept your terms."

Phoe could barely contain her excitement, motioning with a big thumbs' up and matching smile to let

Charlotte know a sweet deal was going down. "Okay. So, just to be clear, you're accepting the entire contract terms we discussed yesterday, right? Including erasing my recent debt and giving me a no limit credit card? Oh, and one last thing. I get to choose who goes with me as I see fit."

"Yes."

Phoe placed her hand over the phone to keep from squealing, turning to Charlotte. "What else should I ask for?"

"Dear, have you heard the fable of the 'Fox and the Grapes'?"

Phoe rolled her eyes and resumed the phone conversation. "What about my finder's fee?"

That one earned a long silence on the other end of the phone.

Shit! Did I just blow it?

The Dog and His Bone fable popped in her head, a favorite of her mother's. Phoe saw herself looking at her own reflection in her mind's eye, holding the original contract. The greedy Phoe decided to override the original deal, and like the dog losing his bone to his reflection in the stream, she now pictured the real contract going poof. To add further insult, her imaginary self smiled smugly and waved playfully goodbye.

"Do you actually believe you can find it?" Simon asked.

Phoe is shocked and relieved, but doesn't dare show a weakness in conviction. "Don't *you* believe I can find it?"

"To be clear." He suddenly sounded hushed and muffled, like he was covering up his handset. "You do know what I'm hiring you to find…don't you?"

"Yes. But why are you hiring me to find something you don't think I can find?"

Her question earned her an extended wait in agonizing silence. The deal was flimsy and getting more precarious by the moment. She decided not to risk it further by asking any more questions. But, before she backtracked with an empty guarantee she could find whatever he hoped she'd find, Simon spoke.

"Good point, Phoe," he said, chuckling, as if he could see her antics over the phone. "All that matters is you are the right person to try and find it. If you can't find it, I'm not sure anyone else can. Anyway, I'll have my lawyer contact you with the paperwork. He'll see you tomorrow morning at nine o'clock sharp, at your store."

She was unsure how to respond, straddling a dangerous line thus far of almost inserting her foot firmly in her mouth.

"Thank you, Phoe. You won't regret this."

He hung up before she could respond, leaving her staring at the handset. Charlotte clapped enthusiastically, and Phoe expected to feel just as excited. But her mind was catching up to her elation, and she realized she had almost too easily agreed to pursue a quest wrapped in ancient myth. A fairy tale. Not usually a good thing, she hoped she didn't soon regret trying to hunt down the Hammer of Thor.

CHAPTER FIVE

Phoe knew the one phone call she needed to make would be one conversation she'd have the most trouble with. Charlotte helped her pack and organize her itinerary, which was always a blessing. Phoe stared at the phone; pondering the last thing she told herself she needed to do.

Planning an unpleasant, but necessary, conversation in her head drained her mentally. Tough to do when she had nearly talked herself out of making the call six times in the past hour. But it needed to be done.

"You know, some things are better done without a plan," Charlotte offered.

Maybe she was right. Phoe smiled at her and moved to another room to make the call in private. She punched in his number and sighed repeatedly while completing a task that suddenly made her fingers feel clumsy. She smiled as she thought he might be away from his phone. He might not accept the call anyway, because....

Phoe prepared to leave her message for voicemail after the fourth ring. She took a deep breath that was cut in half when she heard a click.

"Hello, Phoe."

She could almost see the Cheshire grin he probably had when he saw who was calling him.

"Hello, Peter."

"The answer, my dear Phoe, is 'no'."

"What? How do you even know what I'm going to ask you?"

"I was born at night, but it wasn't last night."

She hated it when he used cheap clichés. "Hey."

"You want the Head of Olmec. I don't think there's anything you could possibly trade me for this little gem."

"I don't want the head," she said. "Well, I do, but that's not why I called."

There was a silent pause, and Phoe hoped he wouldn't be more difficult.

"What do you need from me?" he asked, sounding curious.

"I'm going on a quest for something different." Asking him became harder than she originally anticipated. Her mouth suddenly felt as if it was filled with sandpaper.

"And you want my expertise. I know...go on." The callous, yet simplistic way the words came out of him made her regret this even more.

"All right, damn it! I'm asking you to accompany me on a quest."

"Of course I'll come along."

His answer surprised her as much as it relieved her. The answer was too quick, the agreement too easy.

"You'll have to pay your own way." Her strategy changed to trying to make him beg to join her.

"Knowing you, dear girl, I was planning on it." He chuckled. "What are we looking for?"

"You won't be in charge. I was put in charge and was given the freedom to pick whoever I wanted to join me."

"And you chose me. Yes, yes, we're good on that. So, what are we looking for?"

The more she delayed telling him, the greater the agitation in his voice. No way to get the upper hand.

"The Hammer of Thor." She cringed, eyeing the phone as if it had become a viper ready to sink its fangs into her wrist.

A longer pause of silence, and her belief in the legendary relic's existence began to waver.

"You do realize that Mjölnir doesn't exist, don't you?" Peter said.

"I believed that it *didn't* exist, yes." She tried to phrase her words so she wouldn't discredit the quest and end up with a dial tone on the other end.

"So, you believe it exists now?" His voice betrayed his mischievous grin.

"I'm on a quest for it, aren't I?" she asked, testily.

Another pause.

"You poor girl! Have you seen a doctor? Wait! I know what it is! You have simply lost your mind trying to figure out a way to spend some time with me. You need not play me so desperately, Phoe."

"I'm *not* lying, Peter. I'm going on a fully funded quest for Thor's Hammer and I want you to come with me! Are you in, or *not?*"

"Well, I—"

"No more questions, and no more bullshit!" she interrupted. Losing patience with Peter Kellerman, images of going it alone began replacing the ones with him by her side.

"Very well, then. I'll be there for the duration. No questions asked, except for one. You must give me this one question. After all, I trust you explicitly."

"One question, but then no more after that!"

"What's in it for me?"

She figured he'd ask this from the outset, and it was her biggest hurdle in the vacillating decision to call him up. She had no choice but to relinquish some control of the situation, and she hated having painted herself into a corner. "What do you want?"

"Let me think about it and I'll get back to you," he replied.

She lowered her head and sighed in disgust. "All right, but I will tell you what it *won't* include! Our deal will not include any artifact expedition or artifacts past or present. It will not include giving you any kind of ownership in Simple Treasures, either. And…I will *not* become your wife, concubine, or anything where control over my person is allowed! And…and…." She couldn't think of anything else that repulsed her.

"Fair enough," he said, laughing warmly. "I still need to contemplate the possibilities. Please allow 'compensation' to remain open. Meanwhile, when do we leave? I do need a moment to prepare for a journey that I'm sure will take us to some exotic locale."

She smiled. "Simon Kessler's lawyer will be here at nine o'clock sharp with the paperwork. I was told we're leaving immediately afterward. So, if you can be here, say…ten-ish?"

"Tomorrow morning?"

"Yes."

A longer pause this time. Phoe worried she'd lost him.

"Why did you ask me to come?" He asked, the previous glee absent.

"Uh-uh. No questions asked. Remember, Peter?"

"Ten-ish it is." As she hung up with Peter Kellerman, she thought about how weird it would be to have him along.

She walked into the store to find Charlotte cleaning shelves without any customers around.

"How are sales?" Phoe asked, forcing a smile.

Charlotte shook her head, and went back to cleaning.

"Nothing all day?" Phoe glanced out the front window. The parking area sat deserted. "I thought for sure the King Tut stuff would start moving…eventually."

Charlotte's frown deepened, but then as if she caught herself, she smiled and walked up to Phoe, giving her a big hug.

"Thanks, Char. If I thought that hugs would pay the bills, I'd put yours on the shelves." She laughed.

"You don't want to go there, dear," countered Charlotte, pretending to be serious. "Hugs are free for people who care about each other. Others have to pay."

They both shared a good laugh, and Phoe thought about how good Charlotte had been to her. An even better friend than she'd been to Phoe's mother.

"I've seen some crazy things in my time, but I think you going after the Hammer of Thor beats everything hands down. I wonder what your mom would say?"

Phoe gasped. "Oh shit! I didn't tell her."

"Actually, I wouldn't tell her either, if I were you."

CHAPTER SIX

The next morning, Kessler's lawyer showed up at five minutes before nine. Phoe and Charlotte read and reread everything in the contract. The deal was a little more complicated, since Phoe was required to keep credit card receipts for everything purchased. That was in addition to the usual boatful of legal mumbo-jumbo. But after several run-throughs, everyone was pleased. The lawyer handed her the card once the contract was initialed and signed.

"When can we send the car for you?" he asked.

"You probably should plan on picking me and my associate up around eleven this morning...seeing as he is not here yet."

"I'll make sure to let Mr. Kessler know," said the young attorney, named Jason. He had a nice smile and soft brown eyes. "The car will take you to the Taos Regional Airport where Mr. Kessler's private jet awaits. Thank you...uh...you just used your first initial. What does the T. stand for, Ms. Phoenix?"

"What do you think it stands for?"

"I'm not paid to guess."

"Then I 'guess' that answers the question, doesn't it?" She had made it legal several years ago, where her first initial and her last name would be sufficient as a signature.

Jason smirked and left a copy of the contract with her, and Phoe gave it to Charlotte for safekeeping. He also handed her a cell phone.

"Keep this with you at all times, Ms. Phoenix. It's a direct line to Mr. Kessler. He wants updates on your progress at every step of the way, regardless of whether it seems significant, or not."

"Do you know what the job is that your employer is paying me to do?" she asked, wondering how deeply Jason was involved with Kessler's enterprises.

"As far as the contract is concerned, you're not getting paid, per se," he advised. "There are certain things that I not only do not wish to be privy to, but are none of my business. Sorry."

"A simple 'yes' or 'no' would have sufficed."

Phoe realized not everyone associated with Kessler is going to know her assignment. Still, she intended to make a game out of it. The worst thing would be her being viewed as a laughingstock. She didn't want to be seen as the woman that got conned into searching for an artifact that didn't exist. Kessler was going down with her if that happened. Damn straight.

CHAPTER SEVEN

With her bags packed, all she had to do was wait for Peter Kellerman.

Unsure what to wear, she decided to start her journey in black jeans and a black sweater, with a black T-shirt underneath, in case she started to burn up. She also wore a fanny pack to carry her essentials.

When the clock approached ten-thirty, Phoe began drumming her fingers loudly on an end table. The tea Charlotte made wasn't enough to keep her irritation from rising.

"He's doing this to me on purpose, Char. I can't believe his nerve, standing me up like this!"

"Like he has ever been on time before," commented Charlotte. "He still has half an hour before the car will be here for you. Have you tried calling him?"

"You know I didn't call him!" she fumed. "You think I should call him?"

As the time crept toward 10:40 a.m., Phoe glared at the clock, as if that would magically bring Peter to her door.

"Phoe, dear," Charlotte asked, gently, after arriving with another cup of tea. "What is the worst part of Mr. Kellerman not showing up in time?"

"If and when I go down in history as the fool who went after an artifact that doesn't exist, I want someone else to drag down with me. Peter is perfect for the part."

"Well at least you're not being selfish, dear," Charlotte deadpanned.

When ten-forty-five arrived, Phoe decided to go on without the man who had her property in his possession. She worked out several scenarios where she'd be able to trick Peter into giving her the Head of Olmec. She could never forget the heartlessness he had shown when he put her in a no-win situation. She should've left Jonathan Kessler to his own devices. Maybe he would have survived the pickle he was in.... But, in truth, maybe he wouldn't have. In the depth of her soul she knew if the situation had played out a hundred different ways and Jonathan was in danger, she would've still gone back to save him and lost the artifact she coveted.

10:55 a.m. Phoe gathered her bags without saying a word. She hugged Charlotte, exchanged goodbyes and then she trudged outside. The limousine was already waiting for her, just as the lawyer promised. She took a deep breath as the driver exited the car and rushed over to grab her bags. She watched him set them inside the trunk and then opened the back passenger door, motioning for her to climb inside. She smiled politely, only to have it fade when she saw Peter sitting next to the wet bar. Sitting with a glass of Scotch on the rocks in his hand.

"What the hell are you doing here?" she seethed.

He regarded her quietly, wearing a smug look of supreme satisfaction. The very look that had always infuriated Phoe. He smiled as he poured her a drink and then handed it to her. "Appletini slightly cool, correct? Oh, and I was invited. By you, I believe."

"Ooh, I knew you'd say that! You know what I mean! What are you doing *in* here?"

"I got here early and had a wonderful talk with Bob. Did you know he's from Colorado?"

"Who the hell is Bob?"

"Our driver, of course. He showed me this magnificent automobile and then guided me to my favorite part."

"The wet bar."

"Yes, indeed, my dear Phoe. The wet bar."

Dressed in khaki shorts with a matching shirt, his mountain-climbing boots with black socks were a fashion disaster. But, he would be the one most comfortable that day, and she wished she had dressed less constrictively.

Phoe took a sip from her drink, thinking to herself how this skill of Peter's promised a nice back up vocation, should things ever go south for him in the ancient relic recovery biz. She made herself comfortable in the seat facing Peter's. Glaring at him.

"You need a passport for where we're going."

Peter smiled. "Where are we going?"

"Someplace that we need a passport for."

"Well then, it's a good thing that I updated it recently. I have it with me. Thank you for your concern."

The rest of the ride to Taos Regional Airport was a quiet one for the most part. Phoe preferred to think about the first stop, which would be Germany because of what the swastika represents to some people: a symbol of Thor's lightning. The earliest swastika was found in what is now known as Mezine, Ukraine, around 10,000 B.C. If that proves fruitless, India and Iran were next on the list, where other forms of the swastika originated.

What if the swastika is a dead end? Is this the right way to go?

She had never been in this kind of a dilemma before. Then again, she had never chased a fable before. She looked over at Peter, to find him intently studying her. As if he knew the right answer.

"You look frustrated, Phoe."

"What? What are you talking about? No. Why did you say that?" Sounding frustrated, she could feel her face flush. With all of the destination possibilities and everything else pertaining to the Thor mythology, she couldn't keep her thoughts straight. But, she could never admit this. At least not to *him*.

"I assume you brought me along for more than just my good looks," he said, eyeing her compassionately. "Maybe I can help. I know this may seem like a daunting task, but we can work through this together. Even if you don't see it yet, I'm in this with you."

Curiosity was waiting to bust out of him from all sides. She could tell that much, but she still worried about losing control of the expedition. Tell him too much and watch Peter take over. It had happened before....But, in this case where she only had incomplete ideas on where to go and how to start, it increasingly felt like a better idea to let him in, share ideas, and get this thing on a smooth course.

"Okay....There's something you should know about this trip."

His smile was the last thing she expected to see. A look of worry or surprise, maybe. But not his trademark smile.

"You have no clue where to start, do you?"

"Am I that transparent?"

"Sometimes...but is that such a bad thing? If you don't mind, may I say something?"

Phoe nodded tentatively.

"Think about the quest, first of all. Does this Kessler hate you in any way?"

She wasn't expecting that.

"Not that I know of. I mean, he doesn't like the fact I came back empty-handed from the Olmec expedition."

"That was for him? Oh. Sorry."

Not sorry enough to give it back, huh?

"I'm sure that he has more to keep him occupied than to have me running around the world on his dime for revenge." I liked that response, since I still wasn't sure how I felt about Kessler.

"You're probably right. Well then, the next logical question is, how would sending you on a quest for a mythological Norse god's weapon benefit him?"

"He's a billionaire. He's obviously got money to burn on chasing a fantasy."

"I'm serious, Phoe. Just stating the facts here. Simon Kessler is a billionaire industrialist with certain eccentricities. He has asked you to find an object that only comic book enthusiasts believe might exist."

"True…but you and I know that if the Mjölnir actually existed, it would change Norse mythology as we know it. What did people think of Troy before Heinrich Schliemann came along? Just like the mythical Trojan Horse and Helen, all of a sudden, scholars would move the Norse gods into the history books. It could rewrite history!"

Peter's left eyebrow rose slightly, and his sky blue eyes were aglow with excitement.

"Hmmm…maybe there is something to this. I guess we will find out soon enough, although Iran might be a better choice. Too bad Americans are hated there right now….Maybe India, if Germany turns out to be bone dry."

The limo parked next to a private jet near a hangar. Peter and Phoe exited the vehicle while the limo driver loaded their luggage onto the jet. Simon Kessler stood at the base of the stairs. "G150" was painted on the tail wing and "Kessler Enterprises" with his logo covered the side. Peter nodded approvingly, while Phoe fought to not let the fact she was in awe slip through. Not in Kessler's presence.

Kessler waited for them to approach and extended his right hand to Peter.

"So, Mr. Kellerman…have you ever been on a private jet before?"

"I haven't accumulated the funds to start thinking about flying on anything other than first class, Mr. Kessler." Peter chuckled, and Phoe could almost see his infectious charm ooze toward her employer.

"Good answer, Peter," said Kessler, chuckling along with him. "Please, call me Simon."

Seeking to avoid being caught up in the overdose of testosterone, Phoe sought to get a peek inside the jet from where they stood.

"It's a Gulfstream G150. Built more for luxury than speed, but there's plenty of that when needed," said Kessler, watching Phoe's fascination.

"Good to know," said Peter."

"Yes, she is a beauty. Don't let anything happen to her."

"We won't."

"I was talking about Phoe. The plane can be replaced."

Phoe whirled around to see Kessler was watching her, while Peter nodded thoughtfully.

"I'll protect her with my very life," said Peter, turning his attention to the plane.

"Good. See that you do."

The two men watched Phoe board the jet. But a moment later, she ran back down the stairs and headed for the limo.

"No! Hell no!" shouted Kessler as he pursued her to the car. "What's the matter? You agreed and signed the contract!"

Phoe leaned her back against the limo with her arms crossed. Ignoring Simon Kessler, she pointed to the top of the stairs, motioning for Peter to go take a look. He trotted up the stairs and stepped through the open door. It looked quite nice, plush—definitely a rich guy's cushy ride. At one of the tables and regarding him from an overstuffed leather chair was the guy who screwed up Phoe's last trip.

"Hello, Peter," said Jonathan Kessler. "How nice to see you again...you cheating asshole!"

Chapter Eight

Phoe glared at Simon Kessler, not buying a damned thing he said as he tried to explain why his son is on the jet.

"Phoe. I know you believe that Jonathan may have been responsible for slowing you down the last time," he said, pleading for her to reconsider her resignation. "I understand that the very sight of him causes you pain. But you have to understand that I need someone other than the pilot to stay with the jet while you and Peter are out and about finding Thor's Hammer."

She made no effort to hide her questioning look.

"He is not joining you on your quest."

Her expression softened…slightly. "Do you give me your word?"

"Absolutely. I give my word that you are under no obligation whatsoever to have my son tag along while you find my hammer."

"We'll see," she grumbled. "But any more unpleasant surprises and I quit!"

A smart, highly successful businessman, he nodded courteously. She hated the look in his eye, though, that spoke to enjoyment of the victory he just won. Like the extra tug-of-war over Jonathan's presence was a nice little bonus. Still, she allowed Kessler to steer her up the stairs to board the plane.

A female flight attendant dressed in a dark blue vest covering a red button-down shirt greeted her when she stepped inside the main cabin. *Why of course!* Phoe thought to herself, noting the young woman's ruffled mini-skirt and Hollywood smile.

"Can I get you a beverage or a menu before we take off?"

"No, thank you…" Phoe's comment trailed off as she took in the plane's opulent interior.

"If you need anything on our trip to Germany, just ask," said the stewardess. "We will stop briefly in New York before continuing on to Frankfurt."

"Well, okay," she said, looking for Peter.

He motioned for her to join him at one of the seats with a laptop connected. Once she buckled herself in, she was delighted to find that she didn't need to wait to be airborne before accessing the plane's WiFi system. Peter had already started the expedition's research about swastika history, and she joined him, focusing exclusively on how the ancient symbol pertained to Thor.

After the flight attendant's safety announcements, the pilot added his advisory over the intercom. It marked the true start of their journey, and the moment wasn't lost on Phoe. For better or for worse, the search for Thor's Hammer had officially begun.

CHAPTER NINE

5:30 a.m. Frankfurt, Germany

"**P**hoe. We're here."

She looked up to see Peter standing over her, yawning. Disoriented, she glanced around the cabin, expecting to see her familiar bedroom and find that everything so far had all been just a dream.

"I don't know how you could have missed Captain Sampras' final announcement. You must have been really tired. You've been zoned out for hours."

"What time is it?"

"Just after five-thirty, Frankfurt time. Set your watch and let's get going. There's a rental car waiting outside for us."

Phoe checked her fanny pack, grabbed her coat, and prepared to leave the plane. Two customs officers were checking Jonathan's and Peter's passports. She got hers out and went through the security checkpoint.

After everyone checked into the country, Peter got into the driver's side of the Jeep waiting for them.

Jonathan started to get in the front passenger seat when Phoe stopped him.

"Listen, you little freak! I don't care whose son you are! You're not getting a chance to screw this up!"

The doughy-faced kid with a perpetual cowlick on the top of his thick head of dark red hair looked as if his mother just scolded him. Phoe realized she had been a queen-sized bitch to him, often, since first meeting him. For a moment, she hated herself for being so gruff with him…but the Olmec relic screw-up made it damned near impossible not to see rivers of red.

"Peter doesn't know how to speak German," he said shyly. "I do."

Phoe looked at Peter, pleadingly. "You don't know German?"

"Neither do you, so what's your point?" He replied, smiling smugly.

She turned back to Jonathan. "You really speak German?"

He nodded.

"Okay…You can go with us, even though your dad promised you would stay in the plane. Get in the back and don't speak unless I tell you to speak. Are we clear?"

His dull blue eyes came alive and he climbed into the back seat. Once Phoe was situated, Peter started the engine and set the GPS for Fulda.

The countryside provided gorgeous views as they made their way to the Rhön and Vogelsberg mountains. An hour passed moving into the higher elevations, until they reached the city of Fulda in Hessen, Germany.

The architecture from centuries completed a breath-taking scene against the backdrop of the picturesque German mountains. With its charming gondolas, the Fulda River flowing through the city was reminiscent of Venice, and the air carried a slight chill. Phoe was thankful they didn't make the trek in winter.

"We're looking for Dieter Rietz," Phoe advised while finding it hard to focus on the task at hand. The city was almost too easy to fall in love with, having a siren affect on them all.

"Do you have an address?" Peter asked, gawking at the scenery, and more than once almost driving off the road.

"No. Just directions. For some reason, there is no address registered," she said. "I double-checked it on the flight and couldn't find anything besides the directions."

The cell phone given to her by the elder Kessler rang inside her fanny pack.

"Hello, Phoe." It was Simon. "It seems you have made your first stop. Germany is a beautiful country, is it not? I actually drove through Fulda in the fall once. Beautiful, but cold as hell."

"Yes, we're here."

"Give me a call when you're done in Germany. Have fun, but remember why you're there."

"That's why I have you to remind me, Simon. Thanks."

She hung up the phone, wondering about the distinct feeling she had of the senior Kessler doing more than just checking up on them. He was acting more like a virtual guide, with obvious access to their whereabouts. She shivered.

Before long, the directions led them to turn off the main road and onto a long driveway leading to a small house surrounded by tall pines and holly bushes. Phoe made a mental note that there wasn't a mailbox. They stopped the vehicle just short of the house. All three got out to investigate, zipping up their coats.

They casually walked up to the front door. When Phoe noticed an embroidered "*Geh weg!*" wicker welcome mat, she asked Jonathan to translate it.

"It means 'go away'. Looks like no one wants us here."

"Like that's ever stopped me before," she huffed. But, when no one responded after five minutes of various patterns of knocking, she changed her tune.

"Maybe no one's home," said Peter, stating the obvious.

Suddenly, the double-click pump of a shotgun resounded from the other side of the door. Surprised, Peter grabbed Phoe and carried her to the grass next to the walk as a loud blast blew a hole in the door. Jonathan cowered to his knees after nearly getting hit by shotgun pellets and flying debris. All three scurried for cover as the front door opened.

An old woman ambled on to the porch holding the rifle that had obliterated much of her door. Jonathan began to whimper when she aimed at the bush he hid behind, but before he could rise and get himself killed,

Peter rushed from the other side and knocked the woman to the porch. He wrestled the gun away while she screamed at him in German while pummeling him with her fists.

Meanwhile, Phoe decided to take her chances with a side window. She badly frightened an old man sitting by a desk facing the window. They both screamed, and Phoe ran back to the front door where Peter was trying to restrain the old woman without hurting her.

"Jonathan? Where the hell are you?"

"I'm over here."

"Where…what in the hell? Quit hiding and get your ass over here and start translating before we all end up shot!"

"Okay…but—"

"Grow a couple and get over here, now!"

Jonathan crept up to the porch while Phoe used universally understood hand movements to assure the elderly couple that they were not there to hurt them. The woman started to calm down, but the man took off running.

"Follow me, Jonathan—you better keep up!"

"I'm trying!"

Good…seeing some anger there. Maybe, just maybe the little Kessler boy will come through….

The smell of burnt cinnamon filled her nostrils as she chased the old guy down a hallway. Along the way, she noticed knick-knacks and pictures from a long-ago era. Several pictures were of old Army buddies playing around as they posed, and each had red armbands on their left arms.

The old man ran into a bedroom. Phoe realized that it could turn into a life or death struggle if he retrieved a weapon, like a Luger or another shotgun from the room, and caution would've been logical. But her instincts told her to bust into the room. The door, fortunately, was unlocked.

Badly frightened, the old man was on his knees before a bed, and his hands were behind his head.

Is he surrendering?

"Talk to him, Jonathan!"

"Okay…but give me a moment…."

From there, it made little sense to her. Gibberish, which embarrassed her since all she knew how to speak was English. She would have to seriously improve in her understanding and use of other languages. Otherwise, she should give up this side of the business and stick to minding her little store in Taos, she realized.

Jonathan mentioned the English phrase 'Hammer of Thor', and the old man's expression changed from fear to recognition. He shook his head and replied to Jonathan's question in German.

"I think he can help us," Jonathan reported to her, smiling with obvious pride for his success. "He is familiar with what you seek, and ready to talk."

CHAPTER TEN

M r. and Mrs. Rietz sat on a flowered loveseat from yesteryear. Peter and Phoe stood nearby along with Jonathan. As it turned out, Dieter could speak a little English. Gerda, meanwhile, was fairly fluent.

"Please forgive Dieter. He has little experience with Americans. Please tell me about Thor again. I have not laughed like this in a long time." She kept her shotgun next to her. But at least she was smiling.

"Mrs. Rietz. I'm glad I was able to amuse you. I did my research and have found out that you are an expert in the swastika being linked to the mythological God of Thunder." Her smile faded.

"You are serious about looking for Thor's Hammer? So, this is not an ordinary inquiry about the Nazis?"

Phoe nodded.

"Well, at least this is different than usual, which makes it intriguing at least. But, I hope I don't disappoint you with not much more than anyone can Google for these days. The swastika has evolved from the Swastik. Most prefer to call the former the Swastik to keep the two separate. Surely you already know the

Swastik has been around for thousands of years. Used most frequently as an ancient religious symbol by the Greeks, it was relied on as a good luck symbol. Didn't bring us much luck in World War II." She chuckled.

"What about the connection to Thor?" asked Phoe, trying to remain patient. Older people rattled off facts at a slower pace than she liked, but she tried picturing Gerda as her paternal grandmother, with whom she had a close bond up until she'd died three years earlier.

She looked at Phoe with curiosity. "Why Thor? Why not pursue the Easter Bunny or Santa Claus?"

"Because this connection goes further than the basic information you've shared," said Phoe, shifting her weight from one foot to the other. "The Greeks influenced the Vikings, who unabashedly took the Swastik and associated it with their god, Thor. Maybe the Norwegians thought they could get one up on the Greeks, who had no counterpart for Thor."

Everyone laughed, including Dieter, once Gerda explained the joke to him in German.

"Well, Ms. Phoe, perhaps both cultures were just as devoted to their gods," said Gerda. But the interesting thing about the Vikings is they took it a step further, creating a secret society based on a magical and metaphysical link between the Swastik and the God of Thunder."

She grew serious and leaned forward on the loveseat.

"What I'm about to tell you, few people know. You came to the right person. Tell no one you received this information from me. There is a dangerous society you need to be aware of: Ragnarok's Chosen."

Peter regarded her suspiciously. "Ragnarok? The Norse equivalent to our Armageddon?"

"Yes. I found out by accident while Dieter was in the military. When he first told me, I passed it off as a fairy tale, told by men who needed a distraction from the horrors of war. You won't find this information on any of your Internet searches."

Phoe took it in, debating whether this would be the next clue to follow up on. It appeared Peter was doing the same.

"Where do we find this Ragnarok's Chosen?" asked Phoe.

"I do not know," said Gerda. "I have told you all I know. That will be three hundred dollars."

"What? Three hundred dollars! For a story that may or may not be true?" Phoe was suddenly livid. *The nerve!*

"You sneak around outside without invitation, and now I have a door to replace," said Gerda. "Unless you would like me to call our local bailiff to help settle this."

"No, three hundred is fine," said Peter, mouthing to Phoe, *at least it's not in euros.* He pulled out his wallet and handed her three Benjamin Franklins.

Gerda checked the bills against the light to see if they were genuine. She nodded approvingly.

"Thank you for your visit. Good luck to you all and be safe out there."

CHAPTER ELEVEN

The three Americans were quiet during the pictur-esque drive down the mountainside. Phoe didn't know what to say to Peter or Jonathan. Knowing she owed Peter three hundred bucks, she decided to use her *hotline* to call Simon Kessler.

"Hello, Phoe. Will you be leaving Germany soon?"

"We're driving to Frankfurt now. I have a question concerning the credit card. Can I get a pin number to extract cash?"

"Why would you need cash?"

"I didn't consider the fact we might have to bribe people for information. Luckily, Peter had the cash for the Rietz couple."

"I hadn't thought of that possibility," he confessed "Use the code twelve-thirty at any ATM....So, what do you know?"

"There's a secret organization called Ragnarok's Chosen, and it's apparently connected to the Swastik and Thor."

"Interesting. Any clue on where to find them?"

"No. Not yet. But we're working on it."

"Did she provide any solid proof of this secret society?"

"No, she did not," said Phoe, beginning to feel like she had made a mistake.

"Did you get a receipt for the three hundred dollars?"

Shit! "No. We didn't get that either."

"Then you won't get reimbursed if you pay Peter. I thought you understood how this works."

"Yes. I do." She looked at Peter, who suddenly frowned—apparently in response to her frustrated look. She smiled weakly.

"Where are you headed now, Phoe?" Simon asked.

"We're going to Norway."

"Sounds like you are on the right track....Excellent! Keep up the good work"

She put the phone back inside her fanny pack and sighed.

"What did Simon say about the money?" asked Peter.

She drew in a deep breath. "Looks like you're screwed as far as reimbursing your money goes. I'm sorry."

CHAPTER TWELVE

Phoe, Peter, and Jonathan reboarded the plane, soon to be headed to Norway.

Though the journey was still a nebulous one, they were getting closer to Mjölnir. At least Phoe felt that way, and she could tell her male counterparts felt the same way.

"Phoe, I'm glad you asked me to join you on this," said Peter, once the pilot had received her instructions to head to Norway, and had filed the necessary flight plan information with the control tower at Frankfurt Airport. "Admittedly, at first I really thought this was a wild goose chase. But, even if we don't find exactly what you're seeking, I am quite intrigued where this will lead. And, believe me—I want to believe the Hammer of Thor is a real thing. So count on me to stick by you through thick and thin—wherever our journey takes us."

She looked at him, training her gaze on his eyes... trying to avoid their hypnotic quality. There was no discernible bullshit there.

"Let's see what you think once we reach our next destination," she said, smiling coyly. "What's the good word, Jonathan?"

Jonathan had been furiously typing on his laptop in quest of her assignment to dig up everything he could about Ragnarok's Chosen.

"I found exactly seven online RPG sites that have groups with the name Ragnarok's Chosen. I can cross-match the groups with the members who are into Thor or the swastika...or both. Gamers like to brag about stuff they're into, especially when it pertains to the game. This includes character names or weapons of choice. I, myself, preferred to use a Wand of Destruction with my Nineteenth-level Chaotic Evil Elf Magic-User."

Phoe fought to remain patient with the younger Kessler's penchant for talking over people's heads. "I appreciate your enthusiasm, Jonathan, but could you please stick to the things that pertain to our mission?"

He smiled sheepishly. "Sorry...I will try to do better as I tell you what I found. I cross-referenced all of the cities that the gamers live in, even considering that some of them may have lied about who they are and where they are for security purposes. Then I did a little hacking into a system I know pretty well, which cross-referenced the games and found out where they really live and who they really are. I have three groups that could be great candidates for the secret society you're looking for."

Phoe grinned, thanking herself for giving the guy a chance to do his thing unfettered by her criticisms. "Great job Jonathan! How come you never told me that you were this computer savvy?"

"You never asked."

He had a point.

"Okay, Here's what I want you to do," she said. "Of the three groups you have chiseled the list down to, I'd like the one that has the most inconsistencies between the fabrications and the truth."

"That sound's easy enough, but if I may ask.... Why?"

"Because gentlemen, the gamer group who has lied the most about who they are, will obviously be the one that has the most to hide."

Her grin widened to a playful smile, and Peter smiled as well, while Jonathan's face turned red from embarrassment.

"Done, Ms. Phoenix," said Jonathan. "Here's the list that stands out with the most inconsistencies in their profiles." He turned the laptop to where she could see the screen. "It's rare that all of the gamers are in the same place, let alone the same city. But these are. All of this group's members are in Hammerfest, Norway."

Phoe tried not to look surprised. "I probably should see if we can get a rental car booked now for our arrival in Oslo."

"Already on it for you," said Jonathan, smiling more confidently, then his face fell. "Sheesh, Hammerfest is over 800 miles to the north, almost to the very top of Norway."

"Glad we've got warm coats," said Peter, chuckling while tipping his latest drink toward Phoe and Jonathan. "Sounds like we'll need 'em."

CHAPTER THIRTEEN

Jonathan's discovery seemed to infect the entire aircraft with excitement. Better yet, in Phoe's mind, they'd spawned further noteworthy discoveries.

"Ms. Phoenix and Mr. Kellerman…you won't believe what else I've uncovered about Hammerfest," he advised. "The German navy used the city's harbor as a base during the war, which is kind of like what that old lady named Gerda talked about. But the entire city was destroyed by the Germans except for a burial chapel, that still stands today, from what the pictures show. The rest of the city was rebuilt, of course. Kinda like the story of—"

"A mythical Phoenix?" Phoe interrupted, playfully.

"Yeah." He laughed. "It's so cool. Just like a phoenix rising from the ashes!"

Peter was watching news feeds on his laptop, and looked up to acknowledge the joke. But then his smile faded as his eyes grew wide.

"Holy shit!…Phoe you better have a look at this."

He turned his laptop toward her, and at first she didn't see what had him so riled up about the business site. But just below a line about the DOW plunging for the third straight day, was a small headline.

Billionaire Simon Kessler Announces Search to Find Mythical Hammer of Thor.

The story went on to describe an interview with Simon Kessler, discussing his deployment of a specialized team of investigators to locate and retrieve the item long thought to be metaphorical only. The text concluded with a line that Mr. Kessler expected to have something astonishing to share in the next two weeks, and perhaps sooner.

The report contained a link to other attendant articles, including a video announcement on YouTube. The trio silently observed the video....

"Good morning. My name is Simon Kessler. Most of you know me as a risk taker and entrepreneur. I am also a charitable man with over fourteen million dollars in donations to worthwhile charities in 2013 alone. I am also a sane man. I have in my hands a certified statement from Dr. Kathryn Klein, who is the foremost authority on mental illness. In it, she states that I am perfectly mentally fit and show absolutely no signs of either the beginning of or any advanced mental illness. Most of you know that I do not, in any way, take lightly anything I become involved with. I always research all projects before I dive in. Those of you who have negative opinions about me surely cannot argue my thoroughness in any and all discoveries pertaining to my whims and projects."

Phoe practically held her breath, and it appeared Peter and Jonathan were similarly mesmerized. Her heart sank at the details, and she prayed fervently he wouldn't say anything to make her feel any more foolish for agreeing to take on this assignment.

"I guarantee that what I am about to tell you is no whim. Some will scoff. Some will laugh. Some will call me insane. Eventually, you all will believe as I do. I am involved with something that, when proven, will change the course of history. When proven, this will also change the worldview of what is true versus what is mere mythology."

"Oh, shit...here it comes," she murmured.

"I, Simon Kessler, being of sound mind and body... am funding an expedition to find something that has been assumed to be nonexistent. My team is following a trail of breadcrumbs across Europe as we speak, a trail that will soon likely lead them to the Hammer of Thor!"

The stream of online viewers' reactions are mixed, but most are less than complimentary. Many of these are laced with enough four-letter words to make her and her companions blush, judging from Peter's and Jonathan's uncomfortable reactions.

The only comment at all kind was the deadpanned reaction in the plane coming from the younger Kessler:

"Way to go, Dad."

CHAPTER FOURTEEN

The jet arrived safely in Oslo.

Jonathan was the first to unbuckle his seat belt, looking around at Phoe and Peter with childlike excitement. But, unlike in Germany, they would have to go inside the terminal to get their rental. And, the confirmation of a suitable SUV took longer than anticipated, and the details weren't finalized until just before arriving at the airport.

By now everyone was quite tired and arrangements had also been made to stay at the Rica Hotel Hammerfest, which seemed like a good idea since it was near the heart of the city.

"Jonathan, you do have the addresses of Ragnarok's Chosen, right?" asked Phoe, as they stepped onto the tarmac from the plane. The late afternoon sun felt good...not too hot, and much warmer than Peter had led her to believe.

Jonathan nodded.

"Good, then let's move out."

She led the way to the terminal, walking briskly since her hunger was beginning to burn. Her mood that was often acerbic to the wrong responses, or questions, would move into a more dangerous mode for Peter and Jonathan if she didn't eat something soon.

Phoe's special cell phone rang as they approached the Avis desk. Despite her better judgment, she reluctantly answered it.

"What do you think, Phoe? I know you saw my announcement," said Simon Kessler, sounding proud.

"Why didn't you tell me you were going to do something like that?" she snapped.

"Why didn't you tell me you were going to Norway? Oh, Phoe, though it was inevitable that you would follow the right path, you and I could throw accusations back and forth all day. Or, we could keep this wonderful show moving."

"Do you have even the slightest clue as to what you did by announcing to the entire world that we're going to find the Hammer of Thor?"

"That's not exactly what I said, Phoe. I said that my team *has set out to find it*," he countered. "Do you want to know the most interesting part of peoples' interpretations of my announcements? People still hear and see what they want to, my dear. They will comprehend what they want, since that's how all of us digest the world around us. Just like your assumption I can't figure out where you're going. I always know your next move."

Her blood started to boil. "Thanks to your need to be in the spotlight, we will now have to be much more discreet heading north to Hammerfest."

Silence for a moment. "Your identities remain secret," he said, coolly. "So, unless you spill the beans about who you are and what you seek, no one will know exactly what you're up to. I suggest you don't put yourself in another pickle, like what happened in Germany earlier today. Could be worse next time."

"As long as you can keep your Howard Hughes newsbreaks to a minimum like he would do, we won't have to worry about a 'worse next time'," she shot back.

"Touché," he said. "You must admit that this quest has raised the excitement level in your rather humdrum existence. I suggest you loosen up and continue on the wonderful path you have carved out for your team. Dare to live a little, Phoe. And, truly, this *is* your team."

Silence from both, Phoe couldn't wait for the call to end. Obviously, this was her team, her responsibility, her paycheck.

"Hey, when am I gonna get—"

The line cut to a dial tone. She put the phone away, and stepped up to the counter. At least the rental agent was nice and respectful.

CHAPTER FIFTEEN

Peter drove with Phoe riding shotgun.

Jonathan had correctly assumed that the back seat was his domain, bringing a slight smile to Phoe. Maps and other papers were scattered all over the seat. Names, addresses, character profiles, and even pictures of every active member of Ragnarok's Chosen. He held a pen in his mouth while attempting to sort the mess.

"I wish you would've done this back at the jet, Jonathan," Phoe chided him, half jokingly.

"I would have, but you kept rushing me," he replied, obviously feeling much more comfortable in her presence. "There doesn't appear to be a leader of the group, which is really strange. We have to go through each profile to find the leader. The first name I'm reviewing is Francis Agnor."

"Right. Well, you've got about twelve hours, if we decide to drive straight through," said Peter. "Hopefully, what we had for dinner will tide us over for awhile, and we can make some serious headway. Maybe we should let Jonathan take the lead with this one, Phoe. He does seem to be the right age and knows a lot about these RPGs."

Phoe huffed and gave Peter a harsh stare. But he was right, and she knew it.

"What's wrong with that idea?" Peter asked. "Do you think a bunch of nerds will believe that an attractive woman or a man as classy as myself would be into this nonsense?"

He laughed. She didn't. Jonathan snickered quietly in the backseat.

But Phoe liked Peter's statement about her being attractive.

Jonathan looked at Peter and Phoe with mock irritation. "Really guys? If only you knew what it's like being able to become someone else online. It's an amazing feeling to kill adversaries and fight people three times your size. Oh, and the graphics keep getting better....You damned well *should* know I'll be playing these games until the day I die!"

"Maybe you're right," said Phoe, glancing at Peter. "We'll send in Jonathan."

They didn't arrive in Hammerfest until almost six in the morning, local time. After checking into their rooms, taking showers to refresh, they grabbed breakfast and headed for the first stop. They were far too wired to find out what would happen next to waste the day catching up on the sleep they lost.

They followed a local map to the closest neighborhood from the hotel, thinking it would take them a day or two to narrow things down. Most of the houses near the harbor were close together. Jonathan seemed much more nervous, now that it was time to perform. But after a pep talk from both Peter and Phoe, he got out of the car and doubled back to the first house on the list. It's where eighteen-year-old Francis Agnor resided. Jonathan glanced back at the car, took a deep breath and knocked.

An older woman with unkempt hair and wearing an apron answered the door.

"*Hva ønsker du?*"

The woman addressed Jonathan in a firm tone that Phoe and Peter could hear clearly from the car. Jonathan motioned for them to join him.

"*Hva ønsker du?*" the woman repeated, once Peter and Phoe joined Jonathan on the porch.

"She just wants to know what we want," said Peter. "I'll take this one. *Min yngre bror og jeg var bare på gjennomreise. Han er interessert i å bli med i den legendariske online rollespill gruppe, Ragnarok er valgt.*"

Phoe's and Jonathan's jaws dropped, listening to Peter speak perfect Norwegian. The woman studied Peter suspiciously for a moment.

He continued, "*Din sønn er Francis Agnor, er det ikke? Min bror Jonatan har vært i korrespondanse med din sønn.*" Peter reached out to slap Jonathan on the shoulder, provoking a smile from him.

"*Han er på den fordømte gravkapell spiller sin dumme spill.*" The woman smiled broadly.

"Do you even need me anymore?" Jonathan asked Peter.

Peter ignored him, keeping eye contact with the old woman.

"*Kan du fortelle meg hvor dette stedet er?*" Peter added excited gestures.

She motioned for him to wait and went back into her house. She returned with a piece of paper with directions written on it. Before saying goodbye, Peter took the paper from her and escorted Jonathan and Phoe back to the car.

"What was that all about, Peter?" asked Jonathan.

"In a nutshell, I told her you have been communicating with her son about playing in their online group, and that we were just passing through."

They both get in the car with Phoe, who was shaking her head.

"Run that by me again?" She was just as lost as Jonathan.

After Peter repeated his advisement to Jonathan, he added, "She gave me directions on how to get to the Ragnarok's Chosen meeting place at some burial chapel."

"I bet it's the same burial chapel I told you about earlier!" said Jonathan, excitedly. "Remember? It's the only building still standing from when the Germans attacked!"

Phoe is not so sure. "Why would the city of Hammerfest allow a bunch of kids to hold their RPG meetings in what I can only assume is an historical landmark?" she asked "I have one more question, as well.

Peter, you said that you told the woman that Jonathan was communicating with her son, right?"

He nodded.

"It was obvious that Jonathan doesn't speak Norwegian. I'm sure she got that, too. What if her son only speaks Norwegian? How would Jonathan have communicated with him?"

CHAPTER SIXTEEN

Early evening in the Hammerfest hills.

Peter slowed the car down when they spotted a small white chapel with a steeple on the roof over the front door. The chapel sat flush against the base of a hillside. Tombstones and wooden crosses populated the chapel's walled churchyard. The place seemed deserted and after parking the car in front, the trio cautiously investigated the area.

"This could be a trap," said Phoe, scanning the area warily. Small houses peppered the hillside, and all looked deserted for the moment.

"You know, Phoe, I'm not one to give into paranoia, but I may have to agree with you," said Peter.

"We might as well check out the chapel." Phoe took a deep breath to muster her courage. "I'll go first."

"Should we all go at once? I mean, what if we all get trapped? Who will run for help?" asked Jonathan.

"Who exactly could you get any help from?"

He nodded to Phoe, and Peter led the way. Phoe was next, followed by a reluctant Jonathan.

"Since I'm the only one who speaks Norwegian, everyone stay close behind me."

Phoe glared at him; hating the fact her mission had for the most part continually become everyone else's. She had earlier suggested an approach similar to the one used in Germany. But, trying to be sneaky and send someone in through the side would likely be seen as hostile.

The chapel's front door was slightly ajar. Peter knocked, but when there was no response to it or his voice, he opened the door cautiously. A raised podium faced several pews. So far, the place was deserted.

"There's nothing back here but a haphazard stack of boxes," Phoe advised, after peering into a small office in the rear of the building. "There's dust on everything in here…even the pews look quite dusty. No one's been here in a long time."

Peter stepped up to the podium. "It looks the same as everything else in here. Hell, even the organ looks like it hasn't been played in a decade." He ran his fingers over the keys, plowing through dust and cobwebs. "If this is a burial chapel, it sure hasn't been in use for quite a while."

Jonathan studied the organ. "A certain note has to be played."

Phoe and Peter looked at him with eyebrows raised.

"Look, I know it sounds really weird, but I know these things," said Jonathan, seemingly uncomfortable at the scrutiny, especially from Phoe. "This is right up my alley. It's what I would do if I wanted to protect my meeting place."

Phoe's patience with the younger Kessler has reached its end. Helpful with the German, she is in no mood for Saturday afternoon kiddee-show bullshit. "How about we pursue a different idea, boys? Before we start pressing keys that might wake more than the dead, I say we check the floor for hollow sounds. We might not have much time to mess around in here, so let's get to it and use our time wisely."

It didn't take long to find a weakness in the floor, as soon as they all started kicking and pounding on it. Peter's foot crashed through a hole. Phoe and Jonathan began helping him expand the hole. With a small penlight, Phoe showed the others the remnant of the trapdoor hinges on one side, and a stone staircase beneath the floor.

"Who's game to join me?" she asked, stepping down onto the first step.

"I am," said Peter, echoed by Jonathan.

The stairs spiraled down to a dirt landing. Florescent lights lined the ceiling of a room larger than the chapel above. Crude, recent chalk drawings covered one wall, featuring several figures from Norse mythology. Some were hard to make out, but Thor was easily recognizable to them all. A thin glow of light seeped out from beneath an old wooden door at the left end of the wall. Peter knocked on it, adding a Norwegian greeting. No answer. He motioned to Phoe and together they rammed their collective weight into the door and it gave way.

Several young men stood up from a circle of laptops, throwing down headsets that apparently had left them unaware of the trio's invasion. The startled group bolted for an exit near the back of the room, and disappeared into another passageway before she and Peter could stop them.

"We have to catch them before they get away!" shouted Phoe, when Jonathan lagged behind her and Peter.

Running into the passageway, their flashlights revealed it spanned about fifty feet before sloping downward. They were all surprised to find the slope was lubricated, and they were barely able to keep from tumbling down the chute. But when a dozen other young men carrying clubs pursued them from behind, Phoe led the way down, sliding feet first.

Peter and Jonathan tumbled down behind her, landing on a sandy area that marked an entrance to a large cave with its main opening to the outside world several hundred yards away. Jonathan slid into Peter's back and knocked him over. Not sure if it was the wisest thing to do or not, but Phoe pursued fresh footprints in the sand until she saw the dim outlines of the guys who ran from them, running toward the opening.

"Guys, they're getting away!" she hissed, while watching her partners struggle to get to their feet, falling over each other.

But she couldn't afford to wait—her gut urged her on. She ran after the young men, hearing Peter, Jonathan, and the small mob that was also arriving give chase behind her. She could see that the cave opened up into the bay, while the sand was getting damper. Finding it harder to run, nonetheless she picked up her pace.

Phoe started to gain ground on the slowest of the young men running ahead of her, but she would have to catch him soon. It's times like these that she appreciated her endurance training. She couldn't afford to let the guys in front get away. At least not all of them.

The cave opened up to a dock with a couple of speedboats tied to it. Having a clear view of the bay, she saw the other three men untying the boats. Before the last guy could join his buddies, she tackled him to the sand. Surely surprised she was stronger than he, she turned him over and straddled his chest to keep him from moving.

"You better not even think about starting that motor. You need to answer some questions, pal." She played the tough girl, but deep inside she was scared. Not to mention she soon realized from his panicked responses he didn't understand English. *God this sucks!*

Thankfully, out of the corner of her eye, it appeared Peter and Jonathan were closing in. But it also sounded like the other angry guys had disappeared. *Where did they go?* One of the speedboats' engines fired up, and a moment later the boat's occupants scurried away.

Peter stepped up to her and leaned down, sending a tremor through her as he brushed past her chest to become face to face with the man who looked panicked for his life.

"Jeg mener, du ingen skade. Jeg ønsker å tale til Francis Agnor."

The young men stopped and stared at Peter in disbelief. Even crazier, he started to smile.

"I am Francis Agnor," he said. "What do you want?"

"What in the hell?" shouted Phoe in his face. "You can speak English?"

"Yes…but not to a bully girl!" He eyed her defiantly.

"Why you—"

"Phoe, please let me handle this," said Peter.

Unlike what she expected, Peter eyed her compassionately. Damn she was really starting to like this guy!

"Okay," she agreed, and gazed down at the kid claiming to be Frances Agnor. "No funny business from you. Just the truth. Got it?"

"Yes," said Francis. "Will you please get off of me now?"

Phoe relented, and after the four were all standing, Peter spoke.

"We need your help."

"Are you going to harass me like you did my mother?"

"Is that what she said?" Peter replied. "It wasn't our intentions….My friends and I need information."

"You want us to reveal everything about our group? Ha! Try again, American!"

Phoe slapped him, and the annoying snicker turned to tears.

"We couldn't give two shits about your nerd group," she snarled. "All we want is anything and everything you have on the Hammer of Thor!"

CHAPTER SEVENTEEN

"Ha! The crazy American seeks to know of sacred Mjölnir!"

Does this guy have a fetish for physical pain? Phoe wondered.

"This American just happens to be extremely versed in the ways of the Hammer, my friend," said Peter. "The short handle was actually a mishap in the manufacturing by the dwarven brothers who made it. Perhaps it's because dwarves' hands may be thicker than a normal human's; they are smaller in size. *Mjölnir* is translated as meaning *that which smashes*. A more common translation comes from Russians and the Welsh. The combined translation is equivalent to our word, *lightning*. This is one of the reasons some people have tied Thor to the swastika. The arms on the swastika have been mistaken for lightning. Several specimens of Mjölnir amulets have been found all throughout Scandinavia. They're believed to be from the ninth through the eleventh centuries. This simple fact has made several archeologists believe that the Hammer of Thor does, in fact, exist....How was that, Francis?"

The young man stood speechless.

"Now, tell us about the other guys with you….Can they be useful to our research?"

"It depends. Jeremy Riddick isn't involved with our gaming group, but he has organized us into a real group, dedicated to Thor."

"But using the swastika as a symbol?"

"Yes. He said that the New Age has begun with us."

Phoe looks out on the bay with a grimace. "Is he with the guys who sped away?"

"Yes. But I can tell you much of what he has taught us."

"About the New Age of Nazism?" Phoe snickered.

"Yes. But if I show you what I know, you must promise to give credit to Ragnorok's Chosen—our group."

"Sounds reasonable," she said, to which Peter and Jonathan nodded. "Where is it?"

"It's hidden in the chapel above us."

"Great. And how do we get back there? Will your other pals with their bats be prepared to jump us?"

"No…Now that Jeremy has left, they will wait until he comes back," Francis advised. "You won't have to worry until then."

"Well, how do we get back up there?" worried Jonathan, pointing to where we had been unceremoniously deposited in the sand. "We can't go back the way we came, right?"

Francis snickered softly. "There is another passage to take us back to the surface," he said. "Follow me, and I will show you."

CHAPTER EIGHTEEN

Francis led the way back to a narrow passageway near the slide. He pressed against a shaded rock and a slight rumbling announced the rock wall was moving, opening up a stone staircase similar to the one that had taken the American trio to the hidden room of Ragnorok's Chosen. Phoe followed Francis up the stairs, with Peter and Jonathan close behind her, and soon they re-emerged in the secret room with the laptop stations. But everything inside had since been destroyed. A small fire burned in a crate filled with manuals, folders, and what looked like ancient leather bound books, or journals.

"No! All of our hard work! How could he do this?" Francis cried.

They all helped Francis try to put out the fire.

"Who's 'he'?" asked Peter.

"It must be Jeremy….He must have made it back here somehow, or had his gang take care of it," said Francis, despondently. "He has worked so hard on trying to find what you all say you seek. I thought he would be grateful for the help, but he must want the power of Mjölnir for himself only!"

"You said there is stuff hidden upstairs...let's go—"

"It will do no good," he said, interrupting Phoe. "If he destroyed what is here, surely he has either destroyed or taken what is hidden upstairs."

Phoe pulled Peter aside. "I think we can use him. We should take him with us. Besides, it's not like we have anything else we can take from here."

"Do you understand what you're saying? Adding another member to this team may not be such a great idea, Phoe," said Peter.

"He speaks English and he has a great understanding of what we're looking for and where we could find it, if it exists," she countered, trying to keep her voice down since she was getting angry. "Plus, he may truly know what Riddick knows."

Peter shook his head. "Phoe. How will we be able to afford...."

"Leave that to me, Peter," she whispered.

"You're the boss," he agreed, reluctantly.

"Francis. I have a great idea," said Phoe, sauntering over to where Francis stood, mourning over what was left of his customized computer. "Why don't you come with us on our quest? That way you can have an even bigger say, and share, in the recovery of the Hammer of Thor."

Francis hesitated, though excitement danced in his eyes.

"Come on, Francis! You could be a big help! Pleeeeease!" she persisted.

Francis nodded thoughtfully, and a wide smile soon spread across his face. "Okay, I will do it. I will help you find Mjölnir.

Chapter Nineteen

Phoe, Peter, Jonathan, and now Francis prepared to climb into the rental.

"So, Francis, you're really into Thor, aren't you?" asked Phoe.

He looked at her suspiciously. "Yes, I am. I thought we made that clear."

"Oh, we did. I was just wondering why you are drawn to him."

He hesitated, then shrugged and said, "I think it would be the fact that he's incredibly strong and righteous, even without his hammer."

Phoe's demeanor changed, and she pushed Francis up against the car with her right arm jammed against his throat.

Peter and Jonathan were shocked and tried to separate her from him. But she waved them off.

"All right, asshole," Phoe said,. "You don't really know much about Thor, do you?"

Francis panicked. "What? Of course I do!"

"First of all," she sneered. "Thor received his awesome strength from the belt he wore. Second, he had rage problems and a tremendous ego. I believe you're infatuated with the comic book version and not the mythological figure. Your geekiness is showing."

Francis began to sweat noticeably. "What do you want from me?"

"Riddick didn't teach you geeks anything about Thor, did he?" Phoe demanded.

"Well, no, but…."

"He wasn't interested in Ragnarok's Chosen to be part of his new Nazi army and I don't believe he wanted to find Thor's Hammer," she continued.

"I never said we were Nazis!" Francis protested.

"He didn't bother to teach you anything, because there was something that you had access to that he wanted. What *is* it, Francis? *Think!*"

Francis began to hyperventilate. "Jeremy would never betray the Chosen!"

"Just how stupid are you? A guy old enough to be your father comes up from out of the blue and tells you that he's into your little gaming geeks group?"

"Please stop calling us that."

"Think about it, Francis. You have to have some common sense in that brain of yours."

Francis looked disappointed, perhaps realizing that Phoe was right. "Let me go. I'll tell you what you want to know! I swear it!"

She removed her arm from his throat.

"Maybe there is something," he confessed. "When Jeremy first contacted the Chosen, he was interested in our research into underground caverns and sacred meeting places of worshippers. We have found evidence that some underground statues erected to Thor may still exist. He was particularly interested in one legendary underground labyrinth rumored to be real among the Norse god believers."

"Everything you told him about it, you're going to tell us. Now."

"What if you betray us the way he did?"

"We're on the opposing side of Riddick. I think we've established that fact already. But even if we did betray you, you've already given the information to someone who has. You have nothing to lose, and everything to gain."

"Fritzlar, Germany," said Francis.

Phoe urged him to go on.

"Fritzlar, Germany, is where the Thor's Oak tree is…or was. It was destroyed a long time ago, I think in the year 723. They call it Thor's Oak because that was the type of oak tree that has been hit by lightning the most. The funny thing about that city is that it's also the birthplace of the German Empire."

Phoe and Peter exchanged knowing looks.

"Thank you, Francis," she said, "but you won't be needed to come with us after all."

"What? You just take my information and we get nothing in return?"

Phoe took out her cell phone while staring at Francis. After motioning for him to remain silent, she dialed a number.

"Why hello, Phoe. How goes the search?"

"Abnormally well, Simon. We're on our way to Fritzlar, Germany."

"I'll bet you'll appreciate the slightly warmer temperatures there."

"I didn't call to talk about the weather. Since you're going media blitz happy concerning the expedition, I need you to recognize Ragnarok's Chosen located in Hammerfest, Norway. Without them, we wouldn't be going to Fritzlar."

"Interesting. So, you want to share credit with this group?"

"Francis Agnor will be sending all of the names in the Chosen, so I would like an *honorable mention* for them, please."

"Oh, I get it. Of course, Phoe. I will be expecting the email and will make sure to give credit where credit is due. You, of course, will get more of the credit since you work directly for me."

"Of course....Thank you, Simon. Talk to you soon."

She closed the cell phone and took a piece of paper and a pen from her fanny pack. After writing down Simon's email address and her own, she gave it to Francis.

"Here are mine and my client's email addresses. Go ahead and send all of the names in your group so each of you will get credit for helping us."

Almost in tears, Francis eagerly took the paper from Phoe.

"Thank you all. I will get to that right away. Are you really going to try to find the Hammer of Thor?"

She smiled as she and Peter joined Jonathan in the car. "If you believe it exists, then you have to believe that I will find it."

"I don't know if I believe it really exists...or not."

"That's okay," she replied, sliding the rest of the way into the front passenger seat. "We will send you an email when we do!"

Chapter Twenty

Once back in Oslo, and after boarding the jet, Peter kept looking over at Phoe admiringly.

"What is it, Peter? Is my make-up running?" she teased.

"No, Phoe. You look great….I just can't believe how fast you think on your feet sometimes. I was extremely impressed on how you pegged Francis as a lying sack of shit."

"Thank you," she said. "Hopefully, you'll still think that once we're back in Germany on the hunt."

"Oh, I'm sure I will," he said, opening his laptop, apparently ready to catch up on the latest sports news back in the States.

As for her, she found the hum of the jet engines revving up especially soothing. *We are on our way!* She leaned back in her seat and debated on turning on her laptop or not. When she gave in to the urge, after the plane was back in the air, her casual internet search for Jeremy Riddick became more intense…and more frustrating."

"Help," she mouthed to Jonathan, who reluctantly came over to her. "Have you tried different spellings of Jeremy and Riddick?"

"Not yet."

"Being that he is affiliated with Nazism, he probably won't be using his real name, either in real life, or on the Internet. You also want to look for known alliances....How about you use my computer?"

She vacated her seat, and he huffed as he sat down, but started typing.

"Why do you hate me? Is it because I screwed up with the Head of Olmec?"

She cast him a perturbed look that was as playful as his words.

"I don't hate you, Jonathan. At least not any more."

"I know...but you were really upset about not getting the Head of Olmec."

"I'm upset with myself more so, Jonathan. I allowed myself to be put in that situation."

"You pushed me into the water when you knew I couldn't swim."

"You had a life jacket on for Christ's sake!. I knew you would float!" She laughed.

"You're evil," he said impishly. "Here you go."

She looked at the screen over his shoulder. *Jeremy Riddick A.K.A. Jerome Riddick and Jeremy Reddick. Born: 1967 in Bismarck, North Dakota. Father: Arnie Riddick currently in prison for manslaughter/leader of Aryan Brotherhood sect in prison. Mother: Margaret killed by Arnie in crime of passion. No known next of kin.*

Phoe was shocked. "An American, huh? Is there any other information?"

"That's all the access I could get," he said. "I hit a couple of walls that could be a problem. His name may be linked to some federal activity that I couldn't get information about. This guy is big-time bad."

Jonathan returned to his seat, feeling relieved that Phoe hadn't lost her damned mind again. As soon as he had restored his laptop from sleep mode, he decided to visit the Kessler Industries website. A huge animated picture of Mjölnir dominated the upper third of the page, spinning around before flying off. He laughed to himself, realizing his control freak father had spared no expense to exploit the expedition. *What is Dad hoping to accomplish?*

An entire section of the website was now devoted to the quest. Scanning page after page detailed the mythos of Thor, and even what some scientists believe the Mjölnir is made of. When Jonathan reached the last page, he was surprised to see pictures and a biography of Phoe. His father had listed her name as 'T. Phoenix'. Her store, Simple Treasures, was mentioned as well. In fact, the site included several pictures of store items currently for sale, a picture of her assistant, Charlotte, along with the hours of operation and location in Taos, New Mexico and a small map with driving directions.

Next, he turned his search to Fritzlar, Germany, concentrating on places that might be of interest to someone like Jeremy Riddick. Such as Nazi museums and the last-known location of the Thor Oak tree, which was removed in 723. After half an hour of searching the Internet, Jonathan relaxed, stretching his fingers. That's when he noticed a search result for a pub he had passed several times in his initial search, because it didn't seem important. Now it did. An establishment called *Die Bruderschaft*, which translated to English meant 'The Brotherhood'. *What better place to find members of the Aryan Brotherhood?*

CHAPTER TWENTY-ONE

Just before noon, the jet landed at Kassel-Calden Airport.

Phoe, Peter, and Jonathan loaded up their gear. Greeted by a cold breeze, Phoe was pleased that a rental car was waiting for them, as had been the case in Frankfurt. She zipped up her coat to her neck while jogging to the Toyota Camry. *A bit small for our needs, but what the hell, it's free.*

This time, she got in the driver's side and Peter took shotgun. Jonathan mentioned feeling a little cramped inside the back, but when neither Phoe nor Peter respond, he let the matter die.

"You must have this all mapped out, Phoe," quipped Peter. "I'm glad to see the initiative...ready to assume the lead, finally?"

She returned his jab with a condescending look. "Actually, I have no clue where to begin, but I figured if we started just hitting places, we can cover a lot of ground before midnight. We'll still find what we need quicker than we would with you at the helm!"

"Excuse me, Ms. Phoenix," said Jonathan from the back seat. It sounded more like a squeak than an actual human voice coming from the back seat. He held up some pages he'd printed out on the plane.

"Well, Jonathan, if you have an idea, I'd love to hear it. Please call me Phoe, by the way."

"Well, okay, Phoe." She could see his shy smile through the rearview mirror, sending a pang of guilt into her heart. *Gotta work on the charm, Phoe baby.* "I was doing some research while you and Mr. Kellerman rested. I believe the best place to start is a bar called *Die Bruderschaft.* The English translation means 'The Brotherhood'. From what I gathered, mostly from local police reports, it's the perfect place for someone like Jeremy to go."

Phoe smiled slyly at Peter. "The Brotherhood, it is."

Peter asked to see the papers and Jonathan handed them to him.

"I printed out the map, nearby landmarks, and I think everything else we need."

"Thank you, Jonathan. See, Peter, he's not useless."

Peter looked shocked at her comment, and his face turned beet red as Jonathan leaned forward.

"Do you think I'm useless, Mr. Kellerman?"

Peter glared at her, as if shocked he had just been thrown under the bus. Her naughty grin was intended to remind him that she had yet to forgive him for taking the Head of Olmec.

"All right, Phoe, let's get this out in the open....
Turn right at the next stop sign then go straight for
about two miles....Okay, I got the Head of Olmec fair
and square, and I'm really quite tired of hearing about
it all the time. I'm sorry, but it is what it is! Tell me why
you can't let it go!"

She ignored him until she turned right at the stop
sign. "That was the first artifact I actually had a chance
of getting."

"What about the copies of all of the artifacts that
you sell? Didn't you obtain them from the original
artifacts?"

"Of course I did. Otherwise, they wouldn't look
as authentic as they do. The Head of Olmec was...was
going to be the first artifact that I would ever have been
able to call mine."

An uncomfortable silence fell upon the car.

"It's just that Olmec was special," she continued.
"I have gone out on quests before, but that one was
different."

"What about Simon Kessler? Didn't he fund the
expedition? Wasn't he disappointed that you didn't
bring the head back to him?" asked Peter, not near as
agitated as before.

"Yes, but there was a stipulation to our agreement.
Simon wanted to take it on tour for a year. He said he
would have me travel with it, accompanied by a docu-
mentary of me explaining what I had to go through to
bring it back to the States. He told me that after a year

of promoting the hell out of Olmec, he would give it to me." Her voice trembled.

Peter eyed her disbelievingly. "The Head of Olmec? You really believe he would just hand it over like a bag of potato chips?" He mouthed a sorry to Kessler's kid in the back seat.

"Pretty much," said Phoe. "I mean, the notoriety and everything would be cool, but I desired owning a genuine *important* artifact above all else. I'm not greedy like some people...I just wanted one. The Head of Olmec is an amazing piece with an incredible history. I didn't even care about the recognition, really. It would have brought a lot of people to Simple Treasures, though. Would've...."

Jonathan leaned forward to where he peered at them both. "I don't think you have to worry about that much longer, Phoe."

Chapter Twenty-Two

The Camry pulled up to *Die Bruderschaft* at 9:45 p.m. The parking lot was sparsely populated, and the building itself seemed older than most of the buildings in the area. A weathered, blue neon sign of two hands in a brotherly handshake hung over the doorway. One exterior wall of the bar was covered with graffiti.

"What a charming neighborhood," commented Phoe, after parking a block away.

The three get out and casually approach the bar. Phoe felt like a thousand eyes were staring at her from the darkened homes and businesses along both sides of the street. She could tell that Peter felt the same thing, while Jonathan seemed oblivious.

"This bar will probably be host to all kinds of seedy characters," Peter warned.

"Then you should feel right at home," she said. "If not, I'll protect you."

They all chuckled, which felt good to her…to cut the growing uneasiness.

"Don't be so sure of yourself on this one, Phoe," Peter chided, playfully "You might find yourself needing me to protect you!"

They walked up the front steps and entered the bar. The beat of heavy metal music filled the air. And the odor of people who rarely bathe assaulted their nostrils. Only Peter looked like he might not hurl. But politeness seemed like the smartest approach among the room full of frowning, suspicious faces.

They approached the bar, where a few older men leaned without barstools. The bartender was a fifty-ish, overweight man wearing a filthy t-shirt that might have been white at one time. His scruffy red beard looked as if he'd been trying for years to grow it, but only succeeded in making his face look rusty.

The bartender immediately took issue with their presence.

"Bitte nehmen Sie sich die Argumentation nicht!" he snarled.

Before Jonathan could begin to make headway in German, the bartender pulled out a long stick still bearing the bark from when it was found, or torn from a tree. He held it menacingly, forcing the trio to leave.

"Shit! What are we going to do now?" Phoe lamented. Two other rough looking men moved in behind them, guarding the doorway once the trio reached the parking lot. "Well, Peter. It seems like we hit a nerve, just by our presence alone."

Suddenly, her hotline to Simon rang. *Bad timing, Simon!* But with Peter and Jonathan's urging, she took the call.

"What, Simon? *What?*"

"That's the thanks I get for giving you vital information?" said Simon.

"I was in the middle of trying to get information from the locals!"

"Ha! I bet that's going over like a mean, big stick, isn't it?" he said, chuckling. "Phoe, I have information that will rival any dribble you can get from them. You're going to have to learn to trust me. Trust me now!"

Chapter Twenty-Three

Phoe finished her conversation with Simon, trying to take in all the details. Most she managed to retain, but the approach of a familiar face from behind the bar building distracted her. Especially, when the figure carried a sheathed sword.

"We'll have to continue this call later, Simon," she said into the phone, while pointing to the figure now trotting toward them. "Bye!"

"You three have a lot of nerve!" The figure removed the sword, the blade gleaming in the lone streetlight's glow.

Jeremy Riddick's angry face soon came into view. Dressed in a black trench coat, it appeared that he hadn't shaved, bathed, or slept since their earlier encounter. But his blue eyes were on fire, adding to the frightful state of his greased-back hair and ashen complexion.

"Francis told me you were on your way here. How sad that you were foolish to pursue me!" he taunted. "Well, here I am. What the hell do you want from me?"

Phoe shot a wary glance at Peter, and his unsure response told her that they shared the same fear he would rather fight than answer their questions.

"All right, Jeremy," said Phoe, after taking a deep breath. "How did you get here before us? And, what happened with the laptops back in Norway? I was recently informed there was a strong electrical surge through the computer room, as if it was hit by a bolt of lightning."

This announcement caught Peter and Jonathan by surprise.

"Lightning? Where did you get that information?" asked Peter.

"Let me tell you later, please. Just trust me," she whispered to him. "So, Jeremy? We'll start with those two questions and go from there."

Jeremy snickered. "I have access to things you wouldn't understand."

"That's your answer? It's not an answer!"

"Then maybe you would like me to answer you the way you seem to know best."

Jeremy dropped the sheath and held the sword before him in preparation to attack. Meanwhile, the bartender, guards, and a handful of other scowling men crowded the entrance.

"Is this really necessary?" Peter asked, his tone even, calm, and cop-like effective…at least for the moment.

But the others stepped down into the parking lot, armed with clubs and knives. Death was in the air as

Jeremy and his surly German buddies moved in to attack from all sides.

Suddenly, a gunshot rang out, and the ancient sign above the bar entrance exploded. Everyone whirled around to face Jonathan. The barrel of a smoking thirty-eight special was smoking. A thirty-eight special held in Jonathan's right hand.

"Back the hell up! Everyone!" he demanded, motioning for Phoe and Peter to stay close to him.

Everyone backed up except the bartender. As if hoping to call a bluff, the bartender kept walking toward the three Americans.

"I don't think so, fatso!" Jonathan said, cocking the pistol. "Get your lard ass back there with the rest of the rats, or they can clean your bloody brains off their clothes!"

When he kept coming and Jeremy resumed his approach from the side, Phoe seized the moment.

"Where'd you get such a nice big stick?" she asked, seductively. But a moment later, she slid up to him, grabbed him by the shoulder and shoved her knee into his groin. The big bad bartender crumpled to the ground. Then, she had the presence of mind to take the stick, and before Jeremy could lunge at Peter with the sword, she cracked him on the head. He, too, fell stunned to his knees on the asphalt.

"Tell the rest of them to go away," she told Jonathan. "We just need Jeremy, who is going to lead us down into the basement."

"What?" Jeremy had dropped his sword, which Peter kicked away once the rest of the patrons returned inside the bar.

"I have information from a reliable source that there is a basement entrance behind the building. Get up…you're going to lead us there, or die trying!"

"Phoe? Are you all right?" Peter asked worriedly.

"I'm fine…just following Simon's latest directive," she explained. "Grab the sword, unless you've got a firearm you've been hiding like Jonathan."

"I kept it inside my backpack, since customs never checked the plane after we boarded it in Taos," said Jonathan. "I've got an extra box of ammo inside my computer's battery compartment."

"Good boy."

Phoe smiled confidently as she led the way back behind the bar.

Peter and Jonathan seemed surprised by the sudden surge in her to take charge, though they had both seen it in the hostile jungle territory. Maybe she viewed this place like an urban jungle, reasoned Peter. He gripped the ear of Jeremy, who grimaced in pain. But the shit-head soon learned that Peter wouldn't make the pain excruciating as long as Jeremy didn't put up a fight.

"Be ready for anything," Phoe told them, as they came upon a waist-high doorway.

"Is this going to take us into a dungeon or that labyrinth that I read about?" asked Jonathan.

"I hope this just leads to paydirt." She said. "Anything else will be icing on the cake. Are we ready for this, guys?"

"Yep," said Peter, and echoed by Jonathan. A sharp squeeze to the ear got an enthusiastic cry from Jeremy.

As had been the case for most of this trip, the door was locked. Jeremy shook his head when asked about a key. Peter nearly turned him upside down, thinking the miscreant was lying. But, this time it was the truth.

"Very well," she said, launching a deadly kick into the door near its latch. It flung open on impact.

Peter added his flashlight to Phoe's, revealing a spiral stone staircase descending into the earth.

"Well, well." Phoe looked at Jonathan. "It looks like you might get that adventure you're looking for with us. But this is for keeps, this time, Jonathan. There's no way to know what to expect, so stay ready for anything."

The look on Jonathan's face surely told Phoe everything she needed to know. Peter was certain of it—especially when he saw the look of dread on Jeremy's face.

We have definitely come to the right place!

Chapter Twenty-Four

The stairs descended more than twenty feet into the earth. At the base of the stairs stood a sign carved in iron with the words written in German.

"I don't think we'll need your entire translations skills for this one, Jonathan," Phoe remarked.

Jonathan looked closely at the German engraving that read, *Die Bruderschaft der Hammer.* "The Brotherhood of the Hammer? Hmm."

He pulled on the sign and it gave way, surprising her and, from the looks of it, Peter as well. The rock wall in front of them turned ninety degrees to reveal a well-lit corridor. Caution and excitement ran through her core.

Roughly ten foot by ten foot, and likely measured in meters when it was built, the jagged walls pointed to hurried construction. Several large swastikas had been carved into the walls and appeared to run the passageway's length, by her guess roughly a meter apart from one another.

"Frankly, I don't know whether to be impressed by the architect of this place or be appalled by the purpose of its existence," said Phoe, running her fingers across the symbols most recently associated with unspeakable evil.

"A little of each, I'd say," said Jonathan. "Look, Phoe and Peter. It looks like we're headed toward an old wooden door at the end of the corridor."

"I'll take point," she advised. She slowed her pace as they approached the door, and testing the ground by stepping a foot or two ahead to check for booby traps.

They soon reached the wooden door. Phoe tapped on the metal handle to test for any other trap. Nothing happened.

"We're dealing with a Nazi group that has an unusual obsession with Thor, so we're going to continue to take things slow and easy," she said. "I have a feeling that before we're through, we'll be dealing with unexpected electricity in one form or another."

"There you go talking about that shit again," said Peter, from behind, followed by a snicker from Jeremy. "And this asshole is up to his neck in it all!"

Phoe pulled on the handle. Expecting it to be locked or heavy, she was surprised when the door opened smoothly. She stepped beyond the threshold, and her flashlight's beam landed on a large statue of Thor carved from gray marble.

"Bingo," she said.

Jonathan gasped.

The statue of Thor held its hands in the air as if supporting something above it. Dressed in furs with long hair, Mjölnir was shoved into the deity's Belt of Strength.

"The detail is amazing!" Phoe whispered, reverently.

Standing at least fifteen feet tall, the statue was the centerpiece in the small round room. Just big enough for five or six people. Phoe hoped to keep the door open, but as soon as Peter dragged Jeremy into the room, the door slammed shut.

"Duck!" Expecting a booby trap, Phoe lowered her head, and Jonathan followed suit, as if a spinning round blade would come out of the walls to decapitate them. Nothing like that happened. But Jeremy snickered.

"Boo!" he said.

"Better to be safe, asshole!" she retorted.

But he continued to laugh, until Peter wrenched his ear tighter. The howl turned painful.

Phoe joined Jonathan in examining the statue and, they soon determined that the hammer was sculpted from a different material than the rest of the marble statue. He soon discovered the damned thing was actually *loose.*

"Look, you guys!" He wiggled it free while Phoe and Peter watch, breathless. It moved within Thor's belt along the length of the handle. But it couldn't be lifted out, despite moving at least a foot in either direction. Notches line the length of the handle. "I guess we have to find the right notch."

"Peter, what do you think? What do the notches represent and how are we supposed to find out?"

"Maybe we get unlimited chances to figure it out!" he joked. "Seriously, this is something Jeremy should explain."

But despite the inflicted upgrade of pain to both ears, Jeremy shrieked but would not reveal anything.

Meanwhile, Jonathan returned to studying the statue's hammer and belt. Phoe could tell he was on edge listening to Jeremy's discomfort.

"Maybe the clue is in *what* he's doing," Jonathan observed.

Phoe rejoined him in examining the statue for a few minutes. When Phoe walked around the statue in search of some other clue, suddenly a loud rumble shook the ground below them. Sand began pouring down upon them from several sizable holes in the ceiling.

"Uh-oh," said Jonathan.

"You all have trespassed and ruined everything!" shouted Jeremy "For that, you deserve to die!"

"Hey, speak for yourself asshole!" shouted Peter.

"Get him to tell us how to make it stop!" pleaded Phoe.

"I will die first!" Jeremy said defiantly, ignoring fresh, furious twists to his ears. A kick to the gut and a fist to the face did no better.

"Jonathan—help me find a way to slow the sand and I'll try to figure out the puzzle here!" cried Phoe. She took a closer inspection of the hammer and statue. *There's something odd about Thor's positioning.*

The sand had crept up beyond their shins, and Jonathan's asthma had taken him out of the game. *Think, Phoe, think! Think fast!*

When realization hit her, the sand had climbed to their knees. "I've got it!"

"Hurry, please, Ms. Phoenix! I don't want to die!" cried Jonathan, matching the look on Peter's face, while he fought to subdue the maniacal Jeremy.

A sense of calm flowed through Phoe, and she drew upon her own courage in the face of adversity, realizing from here on out she was the *leader*. Their collective fate rested on her shoulders.

"Finish what you said earlier, Jonathan," she told him. "He's holding something which reminds you of what?"

"It reminds me of drowning in sand, Ms. Phoenix!" He was now beyond panicked.

"Concentrate, Jonathan! If we're going to get out, we have to work together!"

The sand was up to their waists. Peter released Jeremy so their captive could breathe.

"He's holding something up! What does that tell you, Jonathan?" she repeated.

Jonathan looked confused...but then his face brightened with recognition. "The tasks! Thor performed tasks that he couldn't do before!"

"Yes, that's gotta be it! And there were three tasks, right?" Phoe grabbed the hammer and pulled it down all the way to the bottom, and then up three notches. The sand immediately stopped pouring in from the ceiling, and the statue started to slide over to one side, revealing yet another spiral stairway heading deeper into the earth. The sand descended into the darkness below.

CHAPTER TWENTY-FIVE

Phoe heard someone or something moving around on the lower level.

She asked Jonathan for the gun and put her index finger to her lips to make sure he didn't make any noise, and Peter kept a muzzle on Jeremy, whose will to fight seemed to have disappeared. *Sensitive ears? Sheesh!* Crouched on the stairs, she could see the lower level without actually going all the way down. A cloaked figure presently struggled to get a piece of the wall to move without success, and whomever it was remained seemingly ignorant of their presence just above. Phoe quietly moved closer to her target, not noticing anything special about the room. Another ten foot by ten foot circular chamber, very similar to the one they had just left, and of course, full of sand. *Shit! There are no obvious exits!*

No doors or any obvious sign that there has ever been a way out of the room, except for the way they came in. She tried not to slip on the sand-covered stairs as she descended with the gun pointed at the mysterious figure. She managed to make it to the bottom with Jonathan right beyond her.

"Freeze!" ordered Phoe.

The cloaked figure stopped pushing on the wall and straightened. The voice said it was a male, and he emitted a menacing chuckle, raising his hands and slowly turning around to face her.

"Interesting. You're not as stupid as I thought."

Holy Shit! "Francis? How did you get here!"

"You're just as stupid as I thought," he said. He motioned to Jeremy who spoke to him in Norwegian. The two laughed. "Did you really think you could stop all of us from protecting what isn't yours to take? Well, I had high hopes we would eliminate you before now. Your perseverance has been an unexpected nuisance. I have no time for you, stupid woman!"

Phoe approached him, determined to hide the powerful rage building inside her. "Hey, asshole. Who's holding the gun? You will make time for us!"

Jonathan and Peter joined them, with Jeremy's arms pulled up behind him to a painful burn by Peter. Jeremy glared at Peter the entire time.

Peter frisked Jeremy and then Phoe pointed the gun closer to Francis's head as Peter frisked him, too, removing a meat cleaver and butcher knife concealed inside his cloak. After handing both weapons to Jonathan, the three of them faced the pair of miscreants.

Jeremy began to laugh nervously, leaning against the wall closest to him and sliding down into the sand with his legs crossed.

"Now, we're all stuck in here!" He whined, running his hands through the sand and watching the granules flow through his fingers.

Phoe looked back up the stairs, and her flashlight confirmed her sudden fear. *The openings have closed? What in the....How?!*

"How in the hell did the room close up without us hearing anything?" asked Peter. The color had drained from his face.

"What, were you expecting Thor to rumble again?" asked Jeremy, chuckling sadly. "Well, it doesn't matter now. You can even shoot me if you want. I've never made it past this room before. Neither has Francis."

"What in the hell is that supposed to mean?" Peter demanded.

Jeremy responded with a blank expression. It appeared all of the fight had gone out of him. "It means that we are all stuck here together for eternity."

Jonathan removed his glasses, squinting as he looked around the room. "I'm not ready to give up."

"Neither am I," said Phoe, moving to the nearest wall opposite the Norwegians. She began touching and lightly pounding on the rough rock. "This is a mistake. It's illogical to make these other secret passageways to just end here."

"Search all you want, but you will soon find it is useless," said Francis.

"Where were you supposed to be going anyway, Francis?" Phoe glared at him while Peter and Jonathan joined in the search for any possible way out.

"I was supposed to be meeting some new *recruits.* We both were. Not that it matters now."

She got in his face. "I don't believe you, you little shit! I think maybe the only truth either of you have told us is that you never made it this far. I think you want us to find the way out for you."

Jeremy's eyes turned black as his anger bubbled to the surface. He stood up and approached her. "I don't give a shit what you and your henchmen think! This is where we are and this is where we'll stay!"

Phoe looked back up the stairs that went nowhere. "Did you know the task challenge right away?"

He turned away from her and sat down again. "Of course. When it comes to Thor, I know almost all of what I need to know. But if you look around you, there is nothing here that I can use my knowledge on."

"Hmmm. You may be right," she said thoughtfully. "Then we just have to look for something else."

The Americans searched the entire room for almost half an hour, to no avail. Meanwhile the Norwegians watched, wearing wan smiles.

There must be something we're missing. Phoe moved up closer to Peter and tried to keep her voice low so only he would hear her. "The room is a puzzle. We're looking at it wrong."

"What do you mean, Phoe?"

"Think about it. There is absolutely nothing extra in this room except for what?"

"Us?"

"I actually thought of that first, but we don't seem to have an affect on the room. If it were the case, don't you think we'd be out by now?"

"Okay," he said, no longer whispering. Even she could see the other three occupant's eyes were locked on the pair as they conversed. "So...you're saying we need to find something that maybe wasn't in here before, but now it is, even though it could apply to us; but it doesn't because we would be out of here by now if it did? Oh, Phoe, now my head hurts."

"I know it sounds crazy, but..." Phoe stopped in mid-sentence as she stared at the top two or three stone stairs nearest the ceiling. She glimpsed the sand that came down from the upper level. *It couldn't be that easy.*

She walked back to Jeremy. "How did you get here before us?"

"You saw me leave in a speed boat. I had a head start. Then you saw me in the parking lot upstairs."

"No. I'm talking about how you beat us here. You beat us to Fritzlar and we were in a jet."

Of course, it took twelve hours to reach the jet, from Hammerfest to Oslo. But her gut instinct told her she was on the right track. So did the guilty look in Jeremy's and Francis's eyes.

Jeremy refused to look her in the eyes any longer.

She persisted, "What about what happened in the Chosen's computer lab? The laptop was destroyed with electricity. It may have even been a lightning bolt."

Jeremy looked up in surprise. "A lightning bolt is a silly thing to have in a computer lab. How could it get there?"

"That's what I'm asking you. I know how to get us out of here. If you answer both of my questions truthfully, then I will get us all out of here. If you don't, then we will suffocate together. In case you haven't noticed, it's getting harder to breathe."

Peter and Jonathan nodded approvingly.

Jeremy looked at all three of them and then back at Phoe.

"We call it Thor's Thunder," he said. "I created it by mistake. It was designed from an ordinary Taser. As you probably know, there are known deaths caused by Tasers used against humans. They are diagnosed with something called 'excited delirium.' This is when the body experiences several side effects from being tased, such as psychomotor agitation, anxiety, elevated body temperature, increased strength and more. It is most common in males with a history of mental illness. Anyway, think of that kind of response, except with anything electrical in nature."

"You're a scientist?" asked Peter, his brow furrowed, obviously struggling to put the asshole and scholar together as one person.

"Somewhat, yes. I have redesigned the Taser to only harm electrical devices. When Thor's Thunder is pressed against anything that needs electricity, the juice not only is able to go into any circuit that it has access to via the initial contact, but the charge actually builds in power and absorbs the energy as it travels to complete the circuit. The electricity gives it more power with every circuit it goes through. Once the circuit is complete, it reaches a critical state and can no longer contain the power it has absorbed. It then not only destroys the last item it goes into, but the resulting feedback causes everything it had gone through to short out with an even distribution. You can't find the point of origin. Once activated, the only way it can be stopped is if you disconnect the next thing in its path to prevent the circuit from being completed. Everything that it had gone through up to that point would still be fried. Do you follow me?"

Jonathan couldn't contain his excitement. "That's frigging amazing!"

"You can even leave after you have placed the initial charge," added Jeremy.

Phoe was impressed, but she refused to let Jeremy see it. "Okay. That may explain the computer lab, but what about being able to beat us here?"

"I can only assume that whatever jet you may use... mine's faster."

"Wouldn't it be better to call it 'Thor's Lightning'?"

"I suppose, but I like the way 'Thor's Thunder' sounds."

CHAPTER TWENTY-SIX

The air became staler and everyone could tell the oxygen was getting scarce at an alarming rate.

Despite being cool when they first arrived, the temperature had steadily risen since being locked in the small room together. Everyone was dripping with sweat.

Phoe climbed the stairs, smiling as she reached where the sand seeped in. She pushed off as much sand as she could. Some of it stuck to her sweaty hands. She made sure to get as much sand on her hands as possible while also cleaning off all of the sand she could see before her.

When finished, she jumped down to the sandy floor.

Jeremy glared at her defiantly. "That was your plan? To add more sand to the sand on the floor? I'm glad that I told you about Thor's Thunder. I can now die in peace."

"Maybe I waited because I wanted to make sure that what you told me wasn't bullshit. But you're telling me the truth. One more thing….Show me Thor's Thunder."

Jeremy proudly pulled out a small device that resembled a Taser that had been tied around his ankle, and obviously missed by Peter's frisk. He placed it against the skin of his arm and triggered it. It emitted a small spark that didn't harm him, even with the sweat on his arm. "See? Harmless to humans."

Phoe took her hands covered in sand and sweat and fiound a random starting point at the base of the wall. She placed one hand in the sand as deep as it would go while keeping her other hand in contact with the wall. Her palm was flush against the wall as she started to follow it. Finding it difficult to keep her balance, she continued this exercise until a rumbling sound emanated from the portion of the wall that she'd just passed. Peter and Jonathan looked on in amazement as one part of the wall descended into the floor, exposing not only a cool rush of air and oxygen, but another corridor.

Jeremy and Francis were just as amazed. "How? How did you do that?"

"You shared your secret. I'll share mine. One thing about basic physics is, you never overlook the obvious. There were no symbols, no riddles, nothing to tell us what to do. You knew that Thor had to accomplish three tasks when you came upon the statue from upstairs. You answered the puzzle quickly, so that you never had the sand fall from the ceiling like Jonathan and I did. The sand didn't start falling until I approached the statue, which told me that we needed teamwork to solve the puzzle, because it was only after both of us approached the statue that the sand poured out. This is a weights and measurement puzzle. I don't know how whoever built this managed to get everything so precise, but they did something so that any extra sand placed in the right place would trigger the next door. The sand had something to do with our freedom. It was easy to overlook the obvious, because in this case, the obvious made no sense."

They nodded thoughtfully while Peter approached the new doorway.

"We have to be especially careful from here on out," he advised. "We have no idea what's next."

Jeremy stood and headed for the doorway. "The least I can do is take point since you saved all of our lives." He carefully headed into the new corridor.

Jonathan followed Jeremy as Peter paused to speak with Phoe, whispering his message so that no one else could hear him. "Nice story. Do you really believe that's what happened?"

"I don't know, Peter. All I know is I had to try something. I admit to being desperate. I had no idea my experiment would work. But since it did, I needed to make Riddick think it was my plan all along. I was scared to death. I don't like being down here, but I dislike something else even more."

"What's that?"

"I don't like not knowing what's next."

CHAPTER TWENTY-SEVEN

Jeremy put one foot on the sandy bed of the corridor. He breathed easier when his foot triggered nothing but an impression in the sand. The two-meters wide corridor led to another wooden door at the end, about fifteen meters away. A swastika graced the door with an engraving of Mjölnir tilted slightly in the middle of it. Along each wall were three small rectangular alcoves. Each appeared to be a mirror image of the one across from it, except for the fact that they each had a different object inside. Starting on the left, the objects were a fox fur, an antique bottle, and an old carpenter's hammer. On the right side, the objects consisted of an old belt, a clay wing, and an old wedding veil.

He watched everyone else looking carefully at every object without touching anything. Phoe also seemed interested in the wooden door.

"It appears there is another riddle. The obvious thing would be to get the hammer as part of the puzzle," he suggested.

"No, I don't think so," she said. "For one thing, a carpenter's hammer and the Hammer of Thor are two different animals." Phoe examined the hammer in the alcove. "Any ideas, other than the hammer? Anyone?"

Peter shook his head, for the moment focused on the ceiling. "I, for one, would like to know where the air in here is coming from. Not that I'm ungrateful, mind you. Also, it appears the wall behind us has closed without much noise."

Phoe spun around in alarm and gasped to see it was true. She saw what Jeremy knew all along: They cannot go back.

Jonathan examined the floor around the wooden door. "I would love to know how the builders navigated around the underground sewer system to avoid detection. It must have taken a real long time. To reroute the path around it."

Jonathan flinched as Jeremy responded aggressively. "The sewer system came later."

Phoe upbraided Jeremy, eyeing him suspiciously. "It's amazing how much you know about the construction of this place and yet, you had no idea how to get past the obstructions; some of which were easy puzzles if you had studied them."

"What, you still don't trust me?"

"Maybe I trust you...maybe not. But I have an idea you're ready for more of what's to come than we are."

"Maybe. Maybe not," Jeremy's mimic was followed by a wry smile. He presently studied the bottle of water. "I think we should see which of these items is directly related to the thunder god. The fur could resemble

Thor's raiment. The hammer could be there to throw us off, because it is not the same as Mjölnir."

"Right. We can eliminate that." Phoe looked at the belt. "This belt could represent the Belt of Strength, but I believe it should be categorized the same as the Hammer."

"Agreed." Jeremy moved on to the clay wing. "This is interesting. I know the mythos of Thor and would be hard-pressed to accept this as anything but an attempt to steer us from the true goal."

Peter laughed while looking at the wedding veil. "What about this? Thor wasn't married, was he?"

Phoe smiled. "Yes he was. Well, in myth, anyway. He was married to Sif and, if I'm not mistaken, they had a couple of sons. The wedding veil could actually represent one of two instances in Thor's life. The marriage to Sif or the time he disguised himself as a bride to retrieve his hammer."

Jeremy was impressed with Phoe's knowledge of the mythological God of Thunder. "I would go with the story of him disguising himself as a bride, because it makes more sense in the context of the kind of riddles we've been getting."

Peter looked relieved. "Well, at least this doesn't appear to be one of those timed puzzles."

"Jonathan, you previously mentioned something about a labyrinth," said Phoe. "I've seen everything but a maze, so far."

"I don't know, Ms. Phoenix. Maybe we haven't hit it yet."

"That's promising. You mean, this could get worse?" Peter looked more pensive than he sounded, as he headed toward the wooden door.

"I'm sure this is just the beginning," said Phoe. "Wouldn't you agree, Mr. Riddick?"

"I would agree." Jeremy felt that Phoe was trying to push him into revealing what he hadn't shared yet. *She is incredibly intuitive!* But he had played this game before and he had never been broken. Never a loss. Ever since he could remember, he would only reveal what he deemed necessary to gain the trust of those around him. "Should we discount the clay wing?"

Phoe looked closely at the artifact. She didn't seem that impressed by the clever reproduction. "I wouldn't discount anything yet. Is there anything in the bottle?"

Jonathan picked up the bottle and emptied it out in the sand. A small garden snake came out and slithered under the door.

Jeremy froze in his tracks. He tried to pretend it meant nothing, and he coyly studied Phoe and Peter's reactions to see if they recognized the significance of the snake.

"I believe this represents the Midgard Serpent," she said, "a creature of unbelievable size and strength. Midgard is the term used for the place where the humans dwell or Earth, as we like to call it. During Ragnarok, or the Norse version of Armageddon, Thor is supposed to battle the Midgard Serpent in a fight to their deaths."

Phoe took the bottle from Jonathan. "So, the bottle represents the Midgard Serpent who just slithered under the door. The fur represents the fur that Thor wore. The clay wing has to symbolize the Valkyrie-like wings that some Vikings had on their battle helmets. I believe, depending upon which source you believe, that Thor wore a helmet with wings on it. The belt symbolizes the Belt of Strength. The hammer is a cheap knock-off of Mjölnir and the wedding veil symbolizes the time Thor was disguised as a bride. That's what we have, which isn't much."

Peter's eyes lit up with a revelation. "What's the one thing they all have in common?"

Jonathan looked perplexed. "They all belong to Thor?"

"No. They are all cheap representations of things from Thor's life!" Phoe seemed impressed with her answer.

Damn it, getting closer!

Jeremy stepped over to the veil. "All of them may represent Thor's life, but this represents Thor's deceit!"

He picked up the veil and placed it over his head then suddenly ran toward the door. Before anyone could react, Jeremy passed through the door as if he were a ghost. He laughed at the thought of everyone else standing in shock, and maybe dire fear as a new slight rumbling moves through the corridor. He can hear the other five alcoves receding back into the wall. Where there were five alcoves, now were five passageways leading out of the corridor. *Ha! But which one to take? Don't tell them, Francis!*

"Well, that sucks." Phoe gazed into each passageway, following her flashlight's beam. "There you go, Jonathan. There's your labyrinth."

"Cool." Jonathan seemed oblivious to the potential danger with which they are now faced. The dilemma of splitting up the group had now become all too real.

"Who is going to take Francis, or should we just leave him?"

"He's the one that will lead us back to Jeremy, and our escape," said Phoe. "You guys guard him, and we will have to explore these options one at a time."

"What do you make of the wedding veil as a device that lets the wearer pass through walls?" Peter asked.

"Your guess is as good as mine," Phoe said. "It defies physics."

"Which one should we take first?" Jonathan sounded ready to move on, and a bit miffed at Jeremy. Understandably so.

Before a decision was reached as to which passageway they should take, a distant thud resounded from the first passageway to their left. Peter listened at the entrance to clarify what could be making the sound. A loud growl echoed toward him.

"What was that?!" Jonathan asked, his voice trembling.

Peter stepped into the passageway next to it, perhaps looking for a way to surprise whatever was moving through the one passage. However, as soon as he moved into the passageway, which had once held the hammer as an alcove, it returned to its original size and position. Worse, no one could follow after him.

"Shit, Peter!" Phoe was repelled backward. "Jonathan, you stay with me!"

"I'm not going anywhere alone! I'm with you, Ms. Phoenix! But what about him?" he pointed at Francis, who seemed just as shaken.

"Please don't leave me here—I will help you in any way I can!" The Norwegian pleaded.

The sound of whatever lurked in the first passageway sounded like it was getting closer. Panicked, Phoe moved to the other side of the corridor, testing passageways until they hit the one that had contained the clay wing. As soon as they entered, a wall appeared behind them where the opening was a moment before. They heard light cries for help from Francis on the other side.

"We can't go back," said Phoe, pulling on his sleeve. "Stay with me and don't slow down, Jonathan! Let's move now!"

CHAPTER TWENTY-EIGHT

Peter wondered how the passageway could produce light, but he was grateful it wasn't pitch black.

He hated being alone. It seemed like he always ended up on his own, whether it was high school, college, retrieving the Head of Olmec, or running into a narrow passage. He always ended up alone. That loneliness seemed to surround him now. Constrictive. Every decision he had ever made had left him alone in the end. He hated the solitude, but never knew how to be with anyone for long. He once thought he loved Phoe, but even that didn't make him feel alive. However, she's obviously made her decision to love her passion of finding relics. There was no room for love and romance…and hell, it would just make things uncomfortable for him, too. He knew she could never return his feelings.

He stopped walking and leaned against a wall. When he was ready to continue, he looked up and was surprised to see Phoe. He rubbed his eyes, because there was no way this could be real.

"Phoe?"

He found himself praying she was really there, because she was the only one in the world who could take his loneliness away. She walked up to him. No sign of Jonathan anywhere.

"Did you get separated from Jonathan?" She just stared at him. She smiled slightly, but the whole situation was just plain weird. "Answer me, Phoe! Where's Jonathan?"

There was something wrong with Phoe's eyes. They were no longer green, and appeared to be golden and glowing. His frustration was steadily building. "Answer me, damn it! I've had it with this roller-coaster ride! You will answer me…."

Or what?

Did he just think her saying that? Her lips didn't move. She moved closer.

What's the matter, Peter? Aren't I what you want? Maybe it's not me you want. Maybe you just want to humiliate me the way I've humiliated you all these years. Don't you get it? You're a sad sack of a man that I keep around when I need something. You're my puppet and my bitch! No matter how many times I abuse and use you, you will come crawling back on your hands and knees to appease me. You know how I feel about you, don't you? I would rather be with Jonathan than you! You're a lame joke!

He was having a hard time processing what was happening. He wanted to believe this was some kind of hallucination, but he couldn't shake the feeling that Phoe would say these things to him if she had a chance. The words hurt. He pictured Phoe having this conversation with him thousands of times, but now here she was performing the speech he'd dreaded for years. He's a confident, successful man. How can he let one person do this to him?

Come on, Peter. Is that all you can do? Just stand there while I take your manhood from you? I control every movement you make. Just when you think you make a decision, that's just me pulling your strings! Ha! You're not even a real man!

He realized, increasingly, that none of this was real.

"Stop it, Phoe! You have no right to talk to me like that!"

She slowed but still crept toward him. Her moves were less and less human. Like an insect....She became fluid and smoother as she advanced. *It's like she can read my mind!* He choked on a strong burning smell that made it hard to breathe. His head was clouded with what was real and what may not be real. Confusion made it hard for him to concentrate. She pushed him against the wall.

He hit his shoulder and it *actually hurt.* "You're not real!" he shouted.

His act of defiance succeeded only in amusing her. *Your mother always wanted a girl, didn't she? She rejected you, Peter. Hated you for the fact that you're a male. Why is that, Peter?*

"Shut up!" He was out of control. Lost it! The barrier between fantasy and reality had become so distorted he didn't even know where he was.

Poor little Peter. Because your sweet daddy cheated on your mother with anyone who would have him, your mother despised all men. That includes you, Peter. You are a follower in need of something to make you feel like a man, but you lack the balls to work for it!

Peter tried to fight the despair, but eventually gave in. The precious release of letting go and letting life beat him up had totally encompassed him. He dropped to his knees in defeat and terrible despair.

You're pathetic....

CHAPTER TWENTY-NINE

Phoe and Jonathan ran through the small passageway. Abruptly, she stopped and Jonathan almost ran into her. She had to stop, because about a foot in front of her was a deep chasm.

The chasm appeared bottomless. She picked up a small rock near her foot and tossed it down the hole. She didn't hear it hit bottom.

"We have a problem, Jonathan."

"Yeah. I see it. So, what do we do now?"

A hissing growl sound was getting louder behind them. The passageway continued on the other side of the chasm, roughly fifty feet away.

"Do you think we can jump it?"

"You first, Jonathan….Let me think about this."

"Ms. Phoenix! There's nothing to think about! We need to do something and quick!"

Phoe remembered that the alcove-turned-passageway they went into was the one with the clay wing. *Maybe we can fly.*

Phoe pushed Jonathan back a little and prepared to take a running jump. She hit the end of the passageway with a head of steam and compacted her body as she left the ledge. She tried to not look down, but she couldn't help it. It seemed as if time slowed down until she made it to the other side. She stood up, shocked at what she just accomplished and realized there was something more to this passageway than met the eye. Or perhaps less than what met the eye.

"Jonathan! You can make the jump! Run and jump! You can do it!"

"I don't know! It's really far! What about the laws of physics, Phoe?"

"Hurry up! There's something behind you that may want you for lunch!"

Jonathan looked behind him and screamed more reminiscent of a young girl than an adult male. He took a running start and jumped. He screamed through the entire jump. He landed short, grabbing the ledge and hanging on for dear life. Phoe tried to help him up, but her right hand was suddenly in tremendous pain. She looked at the other side of the chasm from where they both jumped and saw a pair of red eyes coming out of the darkness. She gazed down at Jonathan.

"Jonathan! Did your father ever tell you there were no monsters?"

"What the hell? Can you help me up, please? And yes, he said there were no monsters!"

"He lied."

CHAPTER THIRTY

Peter put his hands over his ears to block out the incessant verbal battering by Phoe. He just wanted her to shut up! He told her to stop it, but she wouldn't. He told her to stop, but he realized *he* needed to make her stop.

It's up to him—*not* her. It's always been up to him. He always allowed another to decide whether he'd be happy or not. *Not this time!*

It took every ounce of inner strength he had to stand up and face Phoe, who continued to taunt him. To laugh at him without mercy.

"I don't need your approval, Phoe."

Bullshit! Your world is based on my existence!

Peter smiled. "Not anymore. Leave me alone! You don't own me!"

Phoe's eyes started to glow orange and red, like sizzling coals. This new turn of events startled him. He turned to run deeper into the passageway. As he ran, fiery warmth came up fast behind him. He glanced over one shoulder and saw fire spreading quickly through the passageway behind him. He ran faster.

Chapter Thirty-One

Phoe managed to pull Jonathan up to safety.

They ran as fast as they could through the passageway, until they came upon another chasm. This one was a mere ten feet to reach the other side. Compared to the previous jump, this one seemed incredibly easy. The ledge they landed on opened into a wider passageway than before. Thinking salvation could be near, they ran until they came to a dead end.

"Now what?" Jonathan worried.

"Look!" Phoe pointed to four men coming out from a secret passage in the wall. They each wore pendants around their necks. The familiar swastika and Hammer of Thor graced each pendant.

Phoe aggressively approached the men, making it obvious she was ready to do battle. When they didn't heed her warning, she launched into an attack that relied on quick punches and kicks. It appeared she was gaining the upper hand, when a deep male voice resounded from nowhere.

"Do you think they inhaled too much?" asked the voice.

"They came very close," said another similar voice. "Let's try to bring them out of it."

Everything suddenly got blurry around her. When she could focus her eyes again, she found herself lying on a stone table. Strapped down, the men she fought were no longer present. Instead, two men wearing the same pendants stood nearby. Craning her neck she soon discovered Jonathan strapped to a similar table, and the other had Peter confined to it. The struggle to understand what is real versus what wasn't seemed to have been lost.

One of the men appeared to be in his mid-fifties. The other man was Jonathan's age.

"What's going on here?" Phoe couldn't raise her head for long, as she quickly grew dizzy.

The older man approached. He carried a pleasant smile and a calming nature. "There is nothing to worry about. You are safe. As are your companions. As soon as you entered the passageways, you were exposed to a non-lethal dose of a hallucinogenic gas."

Phoe feigned feeling relieved. "Oh, thank goodness. I thought I was going crazy. You can let me go now. I feel much better."

"I'm afraid I can't do that. You've stumbled upon something that can never be seen by anyone's eyes except members of The Brotherhood of the Hammer. I'm glad you speak German, because it is so troublesome to try to understand Americans."

His last statement made no sense to Phoe at all. *Why would he say that? I can't speak a word of German—much less understand it clearly. But, I also understand him perfectly in English....So why would I even wish to speak German?"*

It sounded like Jonathan and Peter were waking up.

Peter groaned. Jonathan sounded as if on the verge of severe panic.

"Excuse me, Mr. Brotherhood person." Phoe smiled sweetly at the older man.

He walked back to her. "What would *Sie gerne meine Liebe?*"

She did a double take. *Did he just mix German and English together?*

"I'm sorry, could you repeat that?"

He looked at her as if he couldn't understand her.

"Was *meinen Sie? Nicht sprechen sie Deutsch?*"

"He's wondering why you don't speak German anymore," said Jonathan.

Phoe forced a peaceful smile. "Jonathan, dear.... Please tell him that we're here to become members of The Brotherhood of the Hammer."

Jonathan cleared his throat. "Are you sure?"

"Yes."

"Okay," he said, drawing in a deep breath. "*Da muss ein Irrtum vorliegen. Wir sind hier, um sich anzumelden Die Bruderschaft der Hammer.*"

The younger man approached Jonathan with the older one close behind. When they arrived at the table they mumbled to each other and did a lot of pointing, first at Jonathan, then at Phoe.

"*Wer sponsert euch in der Bruderschaft?*" asked the younger man.

Jonathan glanced in Phoe's direction. She remained silent, praying Jonathan seized the solo role in this conversation. This was his chance to shine.

"Jeremy Riddick."

CHAPTER THIRTY-TWO

Phoe stretched out her neck and legs as she smiled at Jonathan. She and Peter deferred all of the talking to the Germans to Jonathan.

I still don't understand how I could have understood that German guy!

The two German men waved goodbye as they made their way through a long, winding well-lit rocky corridor. They kept their voices low.

"Spill it, Jonathan. What were they talking about?" asked Phoe.

"Well, I told them what you told me to tell them, and old guy asked who our sponsor was. I told him it was Jeremy Riddick."

Peter chuckled. "Mr. Riddick will be most unhappy when he finds out!"

Phoe shushed him. "You do realize that we are in some serious shit if Riddick is trying to breathe deadly life into Nazism, don't you?"

"Good point," Peter agreed, turning serious again. "Phoe, I'm also concerned about this gas we were exposed to in the alcove corridor. A mere hallucinogen?

Last I checked, there is absolutely nothing on this planet that can cause someone to spontaneously speak and understand a foreign language."

Phoe nodded thoughtfully, noticing a new opening in the room. "A mystery for another time, I'm afraid. We've arrived…I think?"

Jonathan peered into the passageway over her shoulder. "What are you…*holy shit!*"

The small corridor seemed to go on for nearly a mile, opening to a large basin. The rocky ceiling above seemed at least one hundred feet high.

You could put a football stadium in here! she thought.

Peter whistled under his breath. The area was enormous. Phoe stepped onto the marble floor, relieved to be free of a sandy surface. Jonathan and Peter followed. By her count roughly forty men and women dressed in professional overalls appeared to be studying and working on the walls. They all wore the same brotherhood pendant.

In many ways, it looked like an archeological dig. Yet different, too. Some of the workers were trying to dig through the rock with some type of handheld laser, while others continued to take measurements. As the trio walked toward the middle of the cavern, they wore looks of amazement at the detailed painting of Thor battling the Midgard Serpent that had been mostly uncovered by eons of debris. Thor was dressed in fur and donning a metal helmet similar to the Vikings. Right hand pulled back, ready to smash his foe. The gigantic serpent had its mouth open, ready to strike.

The painting looked perfectly preserved and in full color, though aged cracks, or crazing, were evident.

None of the workers paid the intruders any mind. Phoe's eyes darted from person to person, looking for Jeremy. *No sign of the bastard.*

Peter motioned for them to get a closer look at the painting. The group's awed reaction intensified the closer they came to the exceptional masterpiece.

"Who would've thought the brutish vikes could create something like this?" said Peter, admiringly.

Their first steps onto the scaffolding were ignored, so they climbed up on the one closest to the depiction of Thor's Hammer ready to be smacked down on the serpent. The painting of the Hammer was about seven feet long. Phoe ran her hands along the rock reverently. Then she noticed something that made her mouth drop.

"What is it, Phoe?" asked Peter.

Phoe started to tell him, but was distracted by a commotion coming from the corridor entrance. Jeremy Riddick stormed into the cavern, drawing the attention of several workers. He angrily pointed to the trio presently thirty feet above the ground.

She looked down from the scaffold and saw two of the men in overalls arguing with Jeremy Riddick. Jeremy angrily looked up and pointed at Phoe again.

She grabbed Jonathan to get his attention. "I need you to run interference for us!"

"What? How? What do you want me to do?" He anxiously looked to where Jeremy continued to point at them. The previously uninterested workers seemed interested now.

"There's an unoccupied dig area across the way," she said. "Climb down and run over there. Start yelling in German that you've found something big."

"What am I supposed to say I found?"

"I don't know…maybe something about how to use the Hammer?" It sounded plausible…to her.

Jonathan shook his head, doubtfully, but climbed down quickly. He managed to avoid the growing crowd on its way. Meanwhile, Jeremy pointed at Phoe and Peter, and then yelled some sort of accusation in German.

"Hang onto something, Peter. Tightly."

Jonathan looked back to Phoe and Peter, and then yelled, "*Alle! Ich habe den Schlüssel gefunden hier!*"

Everyone in the room stopped to look in Jonathan's direction. He pointed wildly to the dig site and smiled like he'd just won the lottery. Nearly everyone cheered and ran toward him. Everyone not named Jeremy Riddick.

"*Nein! Nein, sie Trottel!*" he shouted in a rage.

But he had lost his posse. He moved stealthily toward Phoe and Peter solo.

"Phoe, whatever you're going to do, it better be now!" Peter warned, seeing the burgeoning malice in their fast approaching adversary below.

Ignoring Peter's urges, she turned her attention back to the painting. She noticed that the painting of the Hammer bore the same notches that the stone hammer had in the statue of Thor. She pressed both of her hands on the third notch from the bottom as Jeremy reached the bottom of the scaffold.

Peter became frantic. "Hurry up, Phoe—he's almost here!"

She continued to press her hands upon the third notch on the painting, moving her hands around the perimeter of the notch.

Jeremy began knocking down the scaffold as an excited crowd gathered across the way around a nervous-looking Jonathan.

"Peter! Grab the gun in my fanny pack!" Phoe advised.

He wasted little time in retrieving the weapon, cocking and pointing it toward Jeremy, who looked up and smiled.

Phoe used the brief reprieve to keep digging in the notch. Her fingers grazed something small in the notch, and when she grasped it again it felt like a tiny pin. Using her nails to pull it out, she soon determined it was a switch of some kind, made of iron. Relying on her gut instinct, she pulled it. The wall began to shake.

The wall's shake worsened and Phoe realized she had likely just made a terrible mistake. *This is it! I screwed it all up, big time!* she thought, and then turned to face Peter, who looked bewildered. "I'm sorry."

He mouthed 'it's okay', and turned to watch the wall disintegrate everywhere, except upon the painted Thor. Huge chunks fall from the wall, crushing the workers below, who flee in panic. A perfect three-dimensional figure of Thor remains. Whoever designed the switch also made sure that whatever person triggered the switch would be safe from the falling wall.

But Phoe's biggest concern was for Jonathan, who couldn't locate a place to dodge for cover in the crowd of workers he had lured just moments ago. A large piece of the wall crashed and rolled toward Jonathan, beyond Phoe's view. She screamed and prepared to dive off the scaffold. Only Peter's strong grasp kept her from serious injury, and perhaps, death.

She closed her eyes and wept, unable to keep from picturing Jonathan ending up like her beloved brother many years ago. She had never forgiven herself for the accident....

"Oh, my God—I killed him!" she cried, collapsing in tears upon the scaffold.

Peter wrapped his arms around her while looking down to the floor below. He didn't see any sign of Jeremy. Just dust clouds and rubble, which was the case everywhere. No sign of life from anyone at all.

Chapter Thirty-Three

Phoe screamed as Peter looked over at her from the stone table where he had been tied down.

Jonathan angrily tried to break his bonds from the stone table where he was held. Both Peter and Jonathan were gagged. Phoe's head was covered with a pair of protective goggles that had been electronically modified. There were wires coming out of them and plugged into a television monitor facing the tables. Everything Phoe had just experienced in her mind had been seen by everyone else. Jeremy stood close by with an older man in a lab coat. One of the pendants hung around his neck.

Phoe sobbed as Jeremy took the goggles off of her. Her eyes remained closed.

"What have you done to her? To us?" Peter demanded.

Jeremy grinned knowingly. "It appears you've all underestimated me. You have no idea what my inventions are capable of. There are several governments of the world, including America, waiting in line for a taste. I have made much more money as a free agent than working as a slave for some corporation! Your employer is a fool for thinking my interests are limited to the Hammer of Thor. There is so much more money to be made in altered states of reality!"

Peter fought in vain to free himself from the bonds. "What kind of reality did we see in that video? One of your warped and limited imaginary landscapes?"

Jeremy stepped closer to Peter's table. "What you saw was her subconscious assumption of how the next events in this story would unfold. It is what she believes will happen. This is not even close, of course. There is no big painting on a rock wall of Thor fighting the Midgard Serpent."

Peter looked confused. "What good will it do to see something fictional going on in her mind? She hasn't been down here before."

"I know. Certain knowledge that she keeps to herself is revealed as the drama plays out. She believes that the *third notch* will again come into play."

"With this kind of technology, you could help people, instead of acting like a prick," Peter chided.

"That would be true…if only I had a desire to help people. I choose to use my gifts for my own purposes. Money is always the best motivator to listen to."

"So, Jeremy…all you care about is starting a new Nazi movement? That's original!"

Jeremy laughed. "Have you not been listening to anything I have said, Peter? *Money* is my motivator! The Brotherhood is paying me top dollar to help them find the secret hideout of the Brotherhood of old."

"How much?" said Phoe, opening her eyes and glaring at Jeremy. "How much are they paying you?"

Jeremy appeared to not know whether to laugh or take her question seriously. "Don't try to play me, woman!"

"I'm not. Smile and get the old guy out of the room so we can talk. We can't jump you because we're tied down."

Jeremy nodded inquisitively and shooed the older man out of the room.

Phoe made a feeble effort to look around the room. "Are you recording our conversation?"

"No, and there's no need for me to lie to you."

"I'm going to ask you one more time, Riddick. How much is the Brotherhood paying you?"

"Not that it is any concern of yours, but they are paying me ten million euros."

Phoe snickered. "Bullshit money! Get me to some kind of communication device and I'll let you know why I ask. I know our cell phones are worthless down here."

Jeremy laughed nervously. "You just want to get revenge on me for invading your mind! It's a trick!"

"Then let me prove you wrong."

CHAPTER THIRTY-FOUR

Jeremy put down the microphone on the radio that he used for situations just like this one.

His face was shocked. When he was a child growing up in North Dakota, he never dreamed he would be in demand. Always a wiz with anything electronic, unfortunately the other children called him a *freak* because he would take the most rudimentary objects and turn them into viable working electronic devices. One time, he rewired the school's intercom system and with the addition of a pocket radio, he could transmit his own messages from anywhere within the radio's broadcast distance. He would be at home and perform his own school announcements whenever he felt the urge.

Now he was in high demand from countries that wished to utilize his genius.

He moved to his laptop with renewed excitement. He put in his secret account information for his Cayman Islands bank account. For a moment, he looked at his account in disbelief. His balance was $3,645,213. There was a deposit about a month ago from the Brotherhood for $3,500,000 for his expertise. The balance had since been raised by almost $30,000,000. He placed his hands over his mouth and started to cry from happiness.

The green light blinked on and off on the radio. His distraction was short-lived as he reached for the microphone.

The voice on the other end had a firm tone to it. "Mr. Riddick, or whatever you call yourself, do you like your new account balance?"

"Yes...Yes, I do, very much."

"Good. This is how this works. You will turn over any patents for the Taser and dream innovations that we talked about earlier. Agreed?"

"Yes, of course."

"Good. As of five minutes ago, you are now a full-fledged employee of Kessler Industries Incorporated, for the term of one full year. You are not allowed to take a better offer, or betray my trust in any other shape or form. And, you may not purposely attack or hinder any employees of Kessler Industries, Incorporated. Agreed?"

"Agreed."

"At the end of the year of your employment, I will have the sole option of continuing our arrangement at no less than what you have been paid already. Agreed?"

"Yes. Anything you want."

"State your full name and that you agree to all of these conditions."

"My name is Jeremy Riddick. I agree to all of the terms set by Simon Kessler."

K.T. TOMB

Both Peter's and Jonathan's eyes were locked onto Jeremy. Both wore shocked expressions. Phoe seemed to be fighting the urge to smile.

Peter turned his head to her. "How did you know Simon would go for it?"

"Because I found someone even greedier than Jeremy," she replied. "Simon has everything to gain on this deal."

Jeremy appeared happy and still in shock. "Do you need anything else, Mr. Kessler?"

"Just a few things that you won't need to repeat. First, my reach is worldwide. If you decide to betray me or even slander me in a public forum, you will be erased as easily as one of your computer programs. Am I understood?"

Jeremy's smile faded slightly. "Yes."

"Smile at the three people you are holding captive."

Jeremy smiled at Phoe, Peter, and Jonathan. Jonathan began to laugh. "Ms. Phoenix, you rock!"

"Okay. I smiled at them."

"Good. Now that you are all working on the same side, I suggest you set them free. Also, you might want to keep watch for your former employers. I'm sure they won't take kindly to you taking their money and running."

"How do you know I will keep it?"

The sound of laughing could clearly be heard over the radio by all in attendance.

"Because that's what I would do if I were in your position. Good day, Mr. Riddick. Make sure you don't get yourself or my other employees killed."

"I won't, Mr. Kessler. I promise."

"Words are easy to say. Prove it by your actions."

Acting as if he feared Kessler could somehow see him, Jeremy freed his prisoners. "We are on the same team now. But, we have a serious problem."

Phoe rubbed her neck as she was released. "You mean the fact that we don't have a map of these secret chambers and there's a possibility that the Brotherhood never finished building their lair, so we might be trapped down here forever?"

Peter and Jonathan looked at her curiously while Jeremy appeared to ponder what she said.

"Okay," he said. "I guess we now have two large problems."

CHAPTER THIRTY-FIVE

Jeremy led the trio to the end of a small corridor, and then waved them to move along with him. Phoe walked directly behind him, followed by Jonathan and then Peter.

"Just how many of the Brotherhood are down here, Jeremy?" She asked, keeping her voice low. "Is Francis part of them, too?"

He didn't answer right away. "Francis is dead. Not everything slithering around down here is imaginary."

"He was killed by the serpent back there?" Jonathan pointed to where he thought we had come from earlier, in the hall of alcoves.

"Yes...but let's move on, shall we? And to answer your first question, Phoe, thirty-one men and twenty-five women."

"Great."

The small corridor opened up into a large room, spanning roughly fifty feet by fifty feet. The Brotherhood's symbols were engraved upon one wall. Just beyond this room, and hidden from their direct view, was another. It sounded like a large crowd had gathered there.

"You better let me handle them," Jeremy advised. "It's safer, since they don't know I'm no longer with them."

"Take Jonathan," Phoe suggested. "He speaks German fluently, too."

Jonathan protested with a look, but seemed to take solace in Phoe's mouthed "Just trust me, damn it!"

As Jeremy and Jonathan left the room, Jeremy said something to Jonathan before grabbing Jonathan's arm to drag him. Phoe realized this was to further sell the notion that nothing had changed since the last time the Brotherhood had seen Jeremy.

In their absence, Phoe and Peter had a quiet look around. The ceiling seemed to be as tall as the room was wide. Several small openings were spaced about a foot apart all around the room, and three bigger portals were lined in a row at the other end of the room. Each one had something written in German directly above it. The first one was *Slutten,* the second one was *Sentrum,* and the last was *Begynnelsen.*

A look of recognition hit Peter as he mouthed the words.

"Phoe. Those are Norwegian names. Here's what they mean…."

Afterward, Peter pushed past her and went out of the room, entering the potentially hostile Brotherhood crowd. She peered around the corner to watch him nonchalantly approach Jeremy and Jonathan. Most of the men pulled out handguns and knives until Jeremy assured them that Peter was harmless.

Meanwhile, Peter subtly told him the 'names in the room' are an older form of Norwegian, and to come take a look. Jeremy feigned being upset, and pushed Peter and Jonathan back into the room, motioning to the others that he would be back after dealing with the distraction.

"Okay, we're going to need to be quick about this, or the Brotherhood will kill us all without mercy," Jeremy advised. "Why is Phoe standing by the portal with *Begynnelsen* written above it?"

"Peter told me this one means beginning," said Phoe.

"As in 'Three tasks'?"

She nodded. "What if we're supposed to do them in the order they are in the Thor myth? Then again, what if something bad will happen if we take the first of Thor's tasks in the order they happened?"

"Follow your gut, Phoe," Peter advised. Both Jonathan and Jeremy nodded their agreement.

That's what she did. She moved to the first portal to the left, and as she did, Peter noticed something smaller engraved around the doorway in Norwegian. "Repeat after me," he told her. "Regardless how it sounds. Okay?"

She nodded for him to continue.

"I know this to be the third Task set out for the God of Thunder, Thor."

She repeated, "I know this to be the third Task set out for the God of Thunder, Thor."

The portal's darkness was suddenly replaced by a silver glow. Silver smoke began rolling out from the portal.

Phoe felt a surge of panic. "Isn't this the task where Thor was supposed to wrestle an old woman and couldn't? Shit! She represents old age!"

"Phoe, have you ever felt that you were getting old, in spite of your actual age?"

"Huh?" She looked at her hands—she was aging by the second. She let out a scream, collapsing to her knees.

Jonathan ran to her aid, grimacing as her hair began to fall out and her smooth complexion mottled up with age spots and deep wrinkles. Men and women of the Brotherhood had by then crept into the room, perhaps intending harm, but became distracted by the aging affecting them, as well. With a wary eye on his former cohorts' condition, Jeremy rejoined his new American partners.

Meanwhile, Peter shook his head compassionately for Phoe. "I'm so sorry, Phoe. I had no idea you thought about aging so much."

Great, she thought. *I am powerless to stop it now!*

In desperation, Peter moved to the middle portal. "I know this to be the second Task set out for the God of Thunder, Thor." He didn't need Phoe to repeat the line this time, and the look on his face told everyone that he was well aware of the demon about to arrive. Hell, the entire room shook with the monster's approach.

Jeremy yelled to him. "What in the hell have you done?! Is that what I think it is?"

Peter frowned while nodding.

Jonathan scrambled back from the portal.

A moment later, the portal was destroyed from within by a giant serpent. It's viper-like head crashed through the barrier and was soon snapping its menacing jaws at everyone close by. Phoe sat on her knees in despair, too tired and pained to move. Her hair had thinned and what remained was white. Her skin had become a sallow patchwork of liver spots and more wrinkles than a rhinoceros, and her hands had become twisted with arthritis.

Thankfully, the bulk of the serpent's body remained stuck inside the portal.

Jonathan bravely returned to Phoe while the serpent retreated. "Please, Phoe! Don't give up—we'll figure out how to bring you back!"

By then, her face had aged more than seventy years. She lifted her shaking head at the retreating snake and then toward the last portal. She hobbled to it and stood slumped in front. "I can guess what the last portal's writing is," she said in an elderly whisper. "Jonathan...go to Peter and try to help him. Now!"

He obeyed and ran to assist Peter, and she turned her attention to the last shot she had of being restored to her youthful state.

"I know this to be the first Task set out for the God of Thunder, Thor." She hobbled backward, and once her geriatric body began to recover, she limped to rejoin the others.

Jonathan came to her, offering to carry her, if necessary.

Her legs steadily became stronger. Her breathing became more controlled, and her hair returned to the full, lustrous blonde it had been before. The muscles in her body were toning with each step. By the time Jonathan reached her, she was the young Phoe again. His eyes were as big as saucers, in shock.

"Jonathan. Do you hear a sound like rushing water?" she asked.

"Yes, I guess I do."

"That's water from the sea."

"Which one?"

"Does that really matter?" she chided.

"No. I guess not."

Everyone's attention was drawn to the last portal, where water rushed in, as if a nearby water main had broken.

Peter and Jeremy rejoined them. Peter had a look in his eye that Phoe recognized from their early days, and although she felt glad to see it, she turned away. Besides, the serpent sounded like it might be preparing to make a return. Its angry roars were enough to get the Brotherhood to scatter.

"I can't swim!" shouted Jonathan, as the water level begins to rise around them.

"Trust me—and Peter—together we will make sure you don't drown," said Phoe, grasping his shoulder and forcing the younger Kessler to meet her eye to eye. "I won't let anything happen to you! Okay?"

He nodded tentatively. In this crazy world of illusion and stretched reality, the water began to rise swiftly. But after getting knocked down and thrown under water, Phoe pulled Jonathan to the surface.

When Phoe took another breath, she could see that since the water's rising, it's taking her and Jonathan up to the ceiling. *This was supposed to happen...there must be a way for it to end, too.* Her mind could scarcely comprehend that a giant snake was drowning in a whirlpool created from a myth. None of it seemed real, except people were dying. But...if they could outlast the serpent's death, it stood to reason that some sense of normalcy would return.

Phoe spotted Jeremy and Peter clinging to a wall where the water's current seemed much more calm. Getting Jonathan to doggy paddle with her, she soon rejoined the others. Jonathan would be safe. So would Peter and Jeremy. Meanwhile the water was beginning to go down, draining through portals except the first one. Until the water could drain completely, she realized they would be stuck there. And who knew what other menace could come for them?

From a distance, it appeared to be blocked. But once Phoe swam underwater to have a closer look, she found no logical reason for the blockage. She rejoined the others again.

"Okay. I'm stumped. Any ideas why the water won't flow back in there?"

Jonathan bravely immersed himself, but returned to the surface before anyone could fall into full-on panic.

"I can't see that well, but from what I noticed and what you told us, Phoe, I might have an idea about what was going on. Isn't the concept of Ragnarok similar to the Christian version of the end of the world?"

Peter looked at him, shaking his head in disbelief.. "I can't believe I missed it…but that might honestly be the connection here, Jonathan."

Jeremy's face lit up; obviously delighted by where the conversation had moved to. "At the end of Ragnarok, there is a World Tree where a man and woman come out to start the world over again. It's supposed to end where the Bible's first chapter begins."

Peter looked at the water, and added his own two cents to what Jeremy revealed. "In the Bible, the world was destroyed by a flood. God promised that the world would never again be destroyed by water. Some say that's why there are rainbows. They say that is God putting his War Bow down."

"I think I've got it!" said Phoe, excitedly. "Fire! The world is supposed to be destroyed by a cleansing fire! We need fire to activate this portal!"

They all looked down at the water and frowned at what appeared to be an impossible task: Bringing fire into the water? Jonathan glanced at the ceiling, where a fissure had been created. "Can someone lift me up while I try something?"

Peter agreed, and so did Jeremy. They moved over to him and while maintaining a precarious perch on a stone shelf, they lifted Jonathan to where he pulled down two rock pieces from either side.

"Flint and sulfur! Ha-ha! It was a lucky guess, but I'll sure as hell take it!" said Jonathan, laughing. He started to strike them together, but then hesitated. "This shouldn't work, but we know much of this is an illusion. I can't swim...but all of you can. Someone needs to take the sulfur and flint down to the portal sand strike them together."

"What? Are you nuts?!" said Peter.

"Maybe he is...but I get what's supposed to happen," said Phoe, grabbing the sulfur and flint from Jonathan. Before anyone could stop her, she dove into the water.

She didn't understand how it would work—it shouldn't be remotely possible. Striking a wet flint rock against sulfur normally would do nothing....Yet, even so, while holding her breath she struck the rocks together. To her delight a spark flashed. To her surprise and amazement, all at once, the entire perimeter of the portal ignited in a strange blue flame.

"Can you believe it!" she shouted loudly, after returning to the surface. Meanwhile,, the water's flow speed increased dramatically as it poured into the portal. *"Oh Shit!"*

Before anyone could prevent it, Phoe was sucked into the portal and disappeared, leaving her three male companions in a panic to save her.

CHAPTER THIRTY-SIX

Phoe was pulled down into darkness, while her screams became mute in the rushing water. Fortunately, the water's force threw her out of the flow and on to what felt like a beach. Gradually the darkness lessened, as a greenish glow from crevices in the surrounding rock walls grew brighter. A cave, though small. She moved away from the rushing water and toward the strange green light closest to her.

The light grew brighter as she approached, revealing a large archway and a stone path leading deeper into whatever place this was.

"Ahhhh, shhhiiiittt!"

Phoe whirled around, surprised to find Peter, Jonathan, and Jeremy thrown on to the beach in the same manner she had been tossed just minutes earlier.

"What in the hell is this place?" asked Peter, standing and looking around at the strange green light.

"I don't know," she replied, motioning for all of them to join her. "This entire experience has been one continuous mind-fuck. But I bet we're getting close to an answer…a resolution. At least I hope so, as I am about to lose it!"

"What if we are about to find the very thing you've come for?" Peter said, gently. Jonathan nodded supportively, while Jeremy rolled his eyes, shaking his head disgustedly.

"It had better show up soon," she said, releasing a low sigh. "The Hammer of Thor had better show itself very soon!"

"We're ready to follow you," said Jonathan. Peter and Jeremy nodded.

She led the way into the pathway that was just wide enough to allow them to travel single file. The strange greenish glow, that was almost like some subterranean worms, had seeped in between the rocks jutting out along every side, illuminated the path—including the passageway's ceiling, roughly fifteen feet above their heads. But soon, a thick black mist greeted them, quickly surrounding them all. It grew so dense that they could barely see one another and they held onto each others' shirts while Phoe continued to lead the way.

Just when she began to panic, the fog cleared, as if reacting to her latest state of mind. They were no longer in the passageway, and now stood in a large empty room. Eight members of the Brotherhood blocked the only visible exit. Something golden glowed brightly in another room just beyond the eight hostile figures, six males and two females.

One of the women stepped forward. "*Ich habe Angst sie werden nicht in der Lage sein, fortzufahren. Sie haben uns viele der Bruderschaft. Jetzt ist Herr Riddick steht mit Ihnen. Er ist nicht erlaubt, die Technik, die wir mit ihm. Dies ist unsere finden."*

The woman's words affected Jeremy and Jonathan, and they looked at Phoe worriedly.

"What did she say?"

"We can't leave here alive," said Jonathan, quietly. "They feel that since Jeremy betrayed them and many have died today, we must stay."

Jeremy slapped the back of Jonathan's head.

"Ow!" Jonathan flinched.

"That's enough!" said Phoe. "Tell them they can't stop us from achieving our goal, and we're not about to stay here. Oh, hell, I'll tell them myself!"

She ran toward the woman who had made the announcement, who pulled out a gun. Phoe propelled herself into the air right before she reached her, kicking her in the chest and taking out two males standing close by. Looking up, she yelled, "Jonathan! Peter! Get in the room behind me! There's something in there!"

Jeremy launched himself into the rest of the Brotherhood. "Run and join Phoe—I'll be there as soon as I can!"

Jonathan and Peter bowled over the other woman, who was of slighter build than the first one. When they caught up with Phoe, all they could do was stop and stare at the same object that had seemingly mesmerized her.

In the middle of the room, suspended roughly ten feet above a chasm was a shimmering golden statue of

Thor with his arms at his sides. A primitive work, it obviously came from the ancient Norse tribes. The statue appeared to be standing on a crystal dais that somehow floated in the air. Lying beside Thor's feet was an object crafted from an unusual type of metal....

"Oh, my God! Is that his Hammer?" whispered Phoe, in awe.

Mjölnir wasn't golden like the statue. But it made sense. It carried a soft blue glow.

Jeremy joined them, and the beaten Brotherhood hovered near the doorway, obviously dismayed when he kicked the pile of guns he took from them into the chasm, keeping one automatic rifle for himself. Peter whistled when, after a minute, a tiny report came back up the chasm that the weapons finally landed on something.

"How do we get it?" Phoe asked the question to no one in particular, but then looked at her companions for the answer. "If we try to jump to reach the platform and miss, or slip...."

"Maybe it's like that movie where they have to do the leap of faith," suggested Jonathan.

Peter eyed him disdainfully. "I would expect more from you than pulling a Hollywood stunt out of your suggestion box," he said, but then smiled wryly. "You're starting to sound like Phoe."

Jonathan grinned at the comparison.

Meanwhile, Phoe mentally pictured various scenarios to try to get to the statue without dying.

Jonathan, Peter, and Jeremy—along with the sullen faces of the Brotherhood gathered in the doorway—stood watching her, as if expecting her to somehow solve the impossible puzzle.

"Wait a moment," she said, reaching for a handful of small change from her fanny pack. Phoe tossed the coins to different areas of the room. The coins disappeared without making a single sound. "Well, I'll be damned…."

The realization hit her hard. *The gas. The machine that invaded dreams. The serpent. The flood….Everything was so fantastic and daunting to overcome, but it didn't stop them from getting this far!*

Phoe looked up at the golden statue and the Hammer of Thor again, just sitting there for the taking. *If only? Yes!*

"It's too easy and the answer's right in front of us."

Peter looked at her questioningly.

Phoe stepped back several feet into the previous room. "Clear a path for me."

"Are you sure about this?" asked Peter, looking increasingly worried as if fully understanding what was about to go down.

"As sure as I'll ever be about this place…sure enough!" she said.

Everyone moved away from the doorway. Phoe took a deep breath and sprinted toward the statue. Gritting her teeth, she worried she wasn't running fast enough.

There's no turning back now!

K.T. Tomb

Leaping off the ledge, she twisted her torso, allowed herself to grab the Hammer of Thor. Catching the handle by her fingertips and picturing herself thrusting the weight of the Hammer in front of her, carrying her to the other side where she tumbled and rolled. But she pulled her hand back at the last moment. The only thing that matched her vision was tumbling to the other side. Her feet dangled over the edge until she pulled herself up, hearing cheers from everyone but Peter.

Confused, he asked, "Why didn't you get the Hammer?"

"It would have been suicide," she told him. "I didn't know how much the Hammer weighs. It could have thrown me off and sent me down into the pit. At that last moment, I realized that life is far more important. Perhaps, that's the theme of this whole underground playground."

"Are you frigging serious?" He laughed. "I mean, that's fine…you mean far more to me, and certainly everyone else, by being alive. But, this is a three-sixty change in thought for you, isn't it?"

"I guess it is," she said shyly. "It seems like every lesson we learned was about deceit or surviving tests that shouldn't have even existed. Lies and hidden truths. I've come to value life *much* more than any treasure."

"Life is the greatest treasure of all," he agreed. "Well, I'll be…."

He pointed behind Phoe, where the wall suddenly faded from view, revealing a staircase heading *up*. They were getting out of there…a lesson learned?

158

"Looks like you're right," said Jeremy, upon joining Peter and Jonathan as they strode to where she waited.

Phoe smiled and led the way up the stairs. The journey to find the Hammer of Thor was over. They would leave empty handed but with a new perspective on life.

CHAPTER THIRTY-SEVEN

The trip back to the United States was a somber affair. Some sadness as Phoe, Jonathan, Jeremy, and Peter quietly discussed what might've been. Unsure what to tell Simon, Phoe ignored the special hotline that constantly rang until the jet landed in Taos.

"It's been a pleasure, Phoe," said Jeremy. I'm staying on board with Jonathan, as we are headed to the headquarters for Kessler Industries. That's where I'll be working...If you ever need anything, I suppose you can contact me there, and I've got your address and number in case I discover something you might find... interesting."

Phoe eyed him suspiciously.

"What? You're the only one who knows how to expertly explore the Internet?" He laughed, to which she nodded sheepishly. "You should try harder to be 'un-findable'.

"I hope you both will stay in touch," she said, giving a goodbye hug to both Jonathan and Jeremy.

They watched her leave the plane with Peter, and waiting for them on the tarmac were two separate taxis.

"Well…I guess this is it, huh?" Peter said.

There was longing in his eyes, and she almost moved to kiss him. Almost. Instead, she reached out to shake his hand.

"Don't treat me like that," he chided, opening his arms for a hug. She consented, and the pair held each other tightly until her shoulders started to go numb.

"Don't be a stranger, okay?" he told her, his eyes watering.

"Don't you either," she said.

It wasn't until she reached the cab waiting for her that she started to weep. But she held it in, until she was safely inside the taxi, and Peter's driver had already left with him in tow.

During the drive back to Simple Treasures, she wondered if it was all just a surreal dream, with some good and some bad….Well past her bedtime, Charlotte was waiting with open arms in front of the store. Phoe hugged her tightly, and then her assistant helped carry her bags inside.

"So, how was the trip?" asked Charlotte, wearing a knowing smile.

"It was…quite compelling."

"Really?" said Charlotte, suspiciously. "Want to talk about it?"

"Maybe later," said Phoe. "I'm bushed and I need to recharge my batteries."

"Okay. Why don't you just wind down and take it easy," said Charlotte. "See you in the morning."

"Yep. Goodnight, Char."

Phoe intended to tell her what she thought was important. What Charlotte needed to know…or what was easiest to tell. Tomorrow. She would tell her tomorrow.

Relieved to be home, Phoe stepped into her TV room to unwind, startled to find Simon Kessler watching a program. He turned to smile ar her, and on the coffee table sat a bottle of champagne, open with three glasses. Two of them half-empty and one was full. Hers.

"Congratulations, Phoe! You were an amazing success!"

She didn't know what to say. "So, I'm not fired for not retrieving the Hammer of Thor? I thought you'd be pissed that I came back empty handed."

Charlotte appeared in the doorway, and Simon motioned for her to step into the room. She winked and handed the day's store receipts to Phoe.

Phoe's mouth dropped open. "How can this be? We made all this money in one week?"

Charlotte nodded, her smile widening. "It's all because of Mr. Kessler's advertising! He mentioned you every time he mentioned your quest. People have been coming from all over to buy our merchandise!"

Phoe looked at Simon questioningly, but he motioned there was more. He placed a large wrapped gift on the table. "I didn't lose any money and your new business rush is your payment from me, for now. Plus, this gift from a friend of yours."

"I don't want it," said Phoe. "I don't deserve it."

"Are you sure?" Simon opened it up for her, revealing the Head of Olmec.

Phoe fought back tears. "That bastard," she whispered. "Where is he?"

"I imagine he is at his home here....Although, he and I have some unfinished business to attend to when he visits me in Van Nuys, in the next few days. You are welcome to come, too, you know."

"Why? What do you want with him or me still?" She hated sounding rude, but the revelations in the last few minutes alone had her head spinning.

"Maybe you would like to get a closer look at this," he said, pulling out a tablet from his jacket. He turned it on. "Wouldn't you like to see this up close and personal?"

"Oh my God!" she gasped.

The Hammer of Thor in all its ancient grandeur sat under soft lights inside an expensive display case.

"It looks splendid in my office, don't you think?"

She stared at the picture, shaking her head. "Is it really the Thunder God's hammer?"

"Well, not exactly," he said, chuckling. "It is a wonderful artifact made in the 1600s and worth untold millions, just from the artisanship alone. But the *actual* Hammer of Thor? If anyone asks you if you found the Hammer of Thor in Germany, just tell them what I've been telling them." He stepped over to the television and turned up the volume.

"Did you find the Hammer of Thor, Mr. Kessler?" Phoe asked, raising her voice.

He leaned in close, and brought his TV persona smile even closer.

"We found…*something*. Something that I might just show you some day…if you play your cards right."

He turned off the tablet and grabbed his jacket, and after nodding to Charlotte, he headed for the door to leave.

"Thank you, Ms. Phoenix!" he called over his shoulder. "I may require your abilities at a later date. So, do keep that phone charged and ready. And, make damned sure you answer it promptly next time!"

She and Charlotte watched him leave, and after he retrieved his rental car and drove away, they said goodnight for the second time that evening. Then she returned to where she had laid the Head of Olmec, next to the TV. She caressed it lovingly with her fingers, lightly tracing the incredible artistry. She wondered about Peter, and why he had given it up so readily. Then she thought about the photograph…the Hammer of Thor sitting inside the protective case in Simon Kessler's office. Lastly, she ran through the two conversations she had with Kessler and Peter in the last hour, and the offer to join them for the 'meeting' mentioned by Simon in Van Nuys.

"This shit's far from over," she whispered to herself, allowing a sly smile to spread across her face. "It's just begun."

The End

Phoenix returns in:

The Spear of Destiny

Phoenix Quest #2
Coming soon!

About the Author

K.T. Tomb enjoys traveling the world when not writing adventure thrillers. She lives in Portland, OR. Please find her at:

Please visit her at www.kttomb.com.
Add her on Facebook.
Add her on Twitter.

Made in the USA
Lexington, KY
12 June 2016